WARRIORS OF
THE RAINBOW

WARRIORS OF THE RAINBOW

A. D. Harvey

BLOOMSBURY

First published 2000
This paperback edition published 2001

Copyright © 2000 by A. D. Harvey

The moral right of the author has been asserted

Bloomsbury Publishing Plc, 38 Soho Square,
London W1D 3HB

A CIP catalogue record for this book
is available from the British Library

ISBN 0 7475 5207 X

10 9 8 7 6 5 4 3 2 1

Typeset by Palimpsest Book Production Limited,
Polmont, Stirlingshire
Printed by Clays Ltd, St Ives plc

I

The weather held stable in May, June and July, but August was the coldest month of a winter which had already lasted since the end of the previous year.

The day they let him out of jail, bubonic plague broke out in Hartlepool.

His first impression was that little had changed during his four years inside. It was colder than a refrigerator of course, but the brightly virginal uniformity of snow covered everything as protectively as a plastic glove. But indoors, in the railway stations and post offices, the seediness was beginning to peep out. That was all he noticed to begin with: a new level of seediness behind the street barricades of snow.

At first he thought his memory had made him idealise Outside, made him imagine that, compared to prison life, Outside was more vibrant than it really had been: made him unprepared for how defeated and turned inside Outside had become.

And then he saw that things really had gone bad. The city was full of burnt-out, boarded-up apartment blocks, blitzed by lightning: now snow-sculpted ruins. The people from these blocks begged outside the supermarkets and those not begging had the beggars' shiftiness in their faces. In the streets there had used to be more traffic: now except for police vans there were no new cars at all.

Power cuts averaged one every seven hours. If the television worked, the news was of floods, epidemics, blizzards. Not the worst of the news of course: just old footage of snow-ploughs clearing roads. Outside every railway station there were notices listing the places where trains would no longer be stopping. The cities of Britain were going out one by one like evening lights. A major newspaper had been closed down after printing a feature which included a map of the quarantined provinces. The existence of new, vaccine-resistant strains of every known bacteriological scourge was a listed secret under the Emergency Powers Enabling Act, the often-cited E.P.E.A.

Also listed was the theory that the epidemics were somehow engineered by the ants.

More currently controversial was the issue of introducing food-rationing.

Sometimes the thermometer dropped another dozen degrees in a night; but on his second night out he heard shouting and gunfire two streets away, and in the morning when he passed the supermarket where he had bought fish-fingers the day before he saw it was now boarded up. And on the boarding was a notice, already damp and peeling in the scudding snow. It said:

METROPOLITAN POLICE

LOOTING IS PUNISHABLE

BY DEATH

Above terraces uniformly snow-white, the lowering clouds seemed imbued with a watchful intelligence.

Every day the snow fell relentlessly, each flake a magical pattern of crystals, unrepeatable and unique, each flake perhaps the soul of an animal, one out of all the millions slaughtered by man since the beginning of time.

By now everybody took it for granted that it was the animals who were somehow the cause of the blizzards and the epidemics.

*

There was a Red Indian prophecy: when the earth is sick, the animals will begin to die. When that happens, the Warriors of the Rainbow will come to save them.

II

The human race had been waging a relentless war against every other living thing on the planet.

When man spread across the continents, ploughing the land and planting his seed, birds and rodents had grown fat in the fields which man cultivated, but later, when man became too numerous, he began to sterilise all the land, and to kill or imprison all the other creatures.

Entire species were liquidated. While the American West was being tamed with axe and plough, the passenger pigeon swarmed in flocks which darkened the sky from horizon to horizon for hours on end: but after three or four decades of massacre between erecting fences and tending the crops, a species that was older than man and as numerous as the rain ceased to exist. For ever.

Other species were enslaved. More than 10,000 years ago the first people in Patagonia subjugated the docile giant sloth, or mylodon, and made these harmless creatures live with them in their cave dwellings, slaughtering them for fresh meat during the long winters when it was impossible to hunt in the bitter snows outside. But the mylodon could not breed in caves: it was both the first species that man enslaved and the first he made extinct. But other animals, the cow, the sheep, the pig, flourished when man protected them against the cruelties of Nature in order to prey on them at his own convenience. The cat, the horse, and most of all the dog, formed extraordinary relationships with man: they became tools. No longer entirely passive, like the cow, their enslavement was an even more central fact in their existence.

Other animals were hunted out of the territories where they had once roamed freely, driven off the fat lands which once had supported them in safe numbers. Finally they were allowed to exist only on sufferance in wild game reserves. Reserves: almost the same word as Reservations, where governments sentenced the Red Indians to starve after their surrender to the Whites.

The reserves were a kind of open prison. Other animals survived in close captivity, under lock and key, behind bars like condemned criminals, guarded by people dressed as policemen, in zoos where humans came to gape and pass judgement on them.

But now the animals were fighting back.

III

In the freezing dark, Imogen's place – a flat above a shop – scarcely seemed to have changed during the four years he had been in prison, except that the burger bar which had occupied the ground-floor premises had gone out of business. He only noticed the fifteen-foot stalactite of ice hanging from the broken gutter overhead after he had rung the bell.

Showered, shat and wiped he had been brought to this house in a mini-cab when they had first let him out of hospital, after the fire. After he had saved Imogen from the flames. He remembered the manic-depressive budgerigar and the furniture that looked as if it had come from furniture warehouses that had gone bust after being adversely reported on by *Which*? 'You've got to behave,' Imogen had told him. 'My mum's really strict and, well, you know, she wasn't *that* keen to have you stay.' She had taken him up to her room, where he was to sleep. It had been tiny: just space for a virginally narrow bed, a chest of drawers, with all the drawers open and girlie underwear foaming out of all of them, a wardrobe the size of a coffin, an upright chair, 'for putting against the door when I wax my legs', a Soul II Soul poster, and a snapshot showing two identical little girls, both of whom looked like younger versions of Imogen. 'That's my twin, Claudia, she was, um, run over when we were eight,' Imogen had explained: but she had taken the photograph away and he had never seen it again.

The front door opened, dislodging the ice that had formed in the angles between the uprights of the doorway and the lintel. Imogen's mother peered at him through spectacles that looked like the same tortoiseshell spectacles as half a decade ago.

'Oh my goodness, I didn't recognise you.'

'I'm afraid it's been a long time.'

'You'd better come in.'

But he could tell from Mrs Campbell's tone that Imogen was not there.

He had only stayed in the Campbell flat two days before Imogen's mother had come downstairs, found them necking in front of the television, and thrown him out. His hands had still been bandaged, he was unable to carry a suitcase or even to grasp a coin:

Imogen had gone back to his place with him. And stayed. Stayed for eight months, until the police had come for him.

He asked:

'Is Imogen here?'

'You haven't heard?'

Her spectacles gleamed in the moonlight. There was a bit too much practised surprise in that 'You haven't heard?', a little bit too much of the old Ethel's-married-now-and-has-twins.

'Heard what?'

'Three years ago. Three years last January. North London Flu, the papers called it – the doctor said it was a kind of meningitis. One day she was fine and the next . . . She couldn't have suffered, it was all so quick.'

She couldn't have suffered?

Her mother was telling him Imogen was dead.

'She's dead?'

'You'd better come in.'

Opposite the end of the street was the cemetery which Imogen had passed every day of her life for six years but had never entered till he took her there, the day after they had released him from hospital, the first of those two days with her family. He remembered how crowded the cemetery had seemed with leaves and light and the shadows of leaves, bluebells and armpit-high cow parsley and the bare shoulders of ivy-encrusted headstones registering in the corner of one's eye every time one moved one's head, looming among the greenery like lurking London louts, and a pile of dog turds on a concrete foot-path, like an abstract artist's frog, spot-lit by a beam of sunlight filtering down from above. He had shown Imogen the mass grave containing ninety-five of the people who had died in the cellars at Coronation Avenue, back in the good old days when nobody had ever heard of *Coronation Street*, or even of *Brookside* or *EastEnders*, and Thursday evening merely meant another German air-raid. Behind the ultra-cheapo municipal monument to Stoke Newington's civilian war-dead was where she had handled his penis for the first time, because he had had to piddle and hadn't been able to do it on his own because of the bandages on his hands. There too he had tried to give her his first kiss that wasn't pretending to be a formal goodnight kiss. 'You're not allowed to,' she had said, 'I mean, all those people lying on their backs staring up, they make me nervous.' 'They don't mind,' he had said. 'How do *you* know what happens after . . .' she had said. And now she was dead too, and the cemetery was frozen in like a photo of Lapland, with the snow piled up above the tops of the railings.

'You'd better come in,' Imogen's mother repeated, trying to conceal her shivering.

'No . . . I didn't know. I kept writing but there was no reply.'

'I remember there were some letters from you. We should have written but you know there were so many things to do and . . .'

And anyway he was in trouble with the police, and so was not the kind of person one wrote letters to.

'I hadn't even guessed,' he said.

The end was not the judge saying four years or the square thud of the cell door closing at his back. This was the end.

'Where's she buried?' he asked over his shoulder as he turned to go. That was the only thing left to ask.

'She isn't.'

He stopped at the kerb.

'They took her body. Some government organisation. Organ transplant scheme.'

As if it was an excuse she added:

'You were always going on at her to be more socially aware. She had filled in a donor card without telling us.'

It was not just that she was dead: there was something else. His lips seemed numbed with Novocain as he framed the words:

'They took her whole body?'

IV

There was a power cut and the street lights were blacked out. The moon was only a defiant pale disc high behind raging clouds.

In the dark the slipperiness of the iced-up pavement demanded all his concentration. It was impossible to think anyway.

They had taken her whole body. An organ transplant scheme.

There had been a rumour about it in jail. More than a rumour. One of the other cons had worked in government laboratories, even extra hush-hush laboratories guarded by policemen. 'The Professor', they called him, with his tousled hair and thick-lensed spectacles. He liked to lecture. Sometimes they threw a table at him, other times they listened.

Once or twice he talked about the most secret

government research programme of them all, the project that was going to leave the entire Computer Revolution far behind: the Calloway Institute.

The Calloway Institute was where they had been working on artificial human brains: artificial human brains transplanted into the bodies of young people killed by mysterious illnesses.

*

The human brain is the only organ in the human body whose cells cannot reproduce themselves. We are born with most of the brain cells we ever have, and from the age of twenty these cells begin to die off at the rate of a hundred a minute, 150,000 a day. As we learn to make full use of our intellect, its foundations are crumbling, pouring away like grains of sand. We only mobilise a tiny part of our intellectual potential at any given moment, because it is dying on us even as we are learning to use it, and most of it exists only as a kind of unfertilised reserve. By sixty so much has been lost that intellectual faculties begin to slow, to clog, finally to disintegrate. For some people it appears the first organ to fail: for others almost the last: though in reality it has been failing since adolescence.

And biologists wondered: what if brain cells could reproduce? What if, instead of dwindling at the very moment its owner was learning to master it, what if the brain could grow?

This was the question which the greatest scientific experiment of the century set out to answer.

A regiment of biochemists and physiologists was gathered from all over the world to build a human brain.

To construct artificially a functioning human-type brain was an achievement of scarcely imaginable complexity. But these scientists managed one step further. The brain they built was composed of cells that had the capacity to reproduce.

The brain was grafted into the body of a young man who had recently died from head injuries sustained while helping the police.

For three years this creature lived in a laboratory, constantly watched, constantly monitored by instruments accurate to the two hundred and twenty-fifth part of the force of Mach nine.

He learnt to speak, to read, to think.

He learnt to lie.

He learnt to control the microcomponents in the instruments which responded to the electrical activity of his brain.

For a year these instruments showed readings which were normal, predictable, hoped for. Even when the creature appeared to sleep, his brain was controlling the readings shown on all the hundreds of dials and gauges and digital displays.

And then the creature announced that his artificial skull was too small, that his migraines were becoming worse, that they must give his brain more space. His brain was growing: they must give his brain more space.

The surgeons opened up his artificial skull.

The brain they had originally implanted had been just like a human brain, only a little smaller because of its capacity for renewal. Like any human brain it had consisted, from above, of two lobes, like two halves of a walnut.

But now there were seven lobes.

V

There had been one or two letters during the first weeks after the trial: one or two letters that were too brief too commonplace too unsatisfactory in the way letters nearly always are, with the everyday phrases stripped of the voice and face needed to make them unique. Knowing she wanted him was more important than her inadequate words. They had been going through the procedures to arrange for her to visit. Then silence.

Disappointment anxiety anger bitterness despair. They were in a scale of progression. He went through the complete cycle every day, as well as a slower-rhythmed deeper-probing more maddened cycle of disappointment anxiety anger bitterness and despair which was measured in months.

Thinking of her all the time. While listening to

the clunking footsteps of the screws on the walkway outside his door. While listening to the coughing. While slopping out his cell. In the food queues. In the exercise yard. In the workshop. In the television room. At night. Not especially at night: it was worse in the morning, facing the prospect of another day, another sixteen hours of dreary imprisoned consciousness without her: sixteen hours, nine hundred and sixty minutes, fifty-seven thousand six hundred seconds, without even one second of knowing that she was thinking of him.

Remembering her. Remembering that first morning in the Campbells' flat, waking up to the pain of his bandaged hands and finding on his pillow half a sheet of lined notepaper with the inscription

IMOGEN ♥s U

and a moment later seeing her at the door, bleary-eyed and biscuity-smelling, wearing a sleeveless nightie and scratching herself high up on the hip in such a way as to show she had nothing on underneath, and a moment after that her mother crowding in after her saying, 'Go and put some clothes on at once. Running around in your nightie. Not in my house. Look at you child. Not in my house,' and Imogen, her long-distance runner's arms and legs somehow a size too large for the rest of her, pouting sulkily and retreating without a second look at him. Remembering her later that morning, nervously adjusting the framed ornithological print showing a Jamaican nightingale that hung in the downstairs hall as she told him for the second or third time, '*You've got to behave.*' Remembering the way she had snuggled up to him on the Campbell front-room sofa, with her adolescent girl's mushy mouth, while her bubble-gum dried on the back-rest of a nearby chair. Remembering her the Sunday of the following week, dressed in only the thread of a tampon that dangled in the keyhole-shaped space between her upper thighs, trying to fry an egg in his kitchen and shouting with annoyance as the sizzling fat splashed her bare skin, while, sobbing faintly through the wall, 'You'll Come Back for Me' played on the record-player in the house next door.

'It wasn't love at first sight,' she had told him once. 'It all happened so fast it was three days before it occurred to me something was happening, and a week before I realised it had a name.' When she had first seen him she had been laughing, the leggiest of a trio of black teenage girls parading in their platform-soled trainers through Dalston Cross shopping precinct: but her laugh had converted itself into an absent-minded scowl when she noticed him watching her: and at that very same moment the entire shopping precinct had split apart with an immense gust of dust and a ripping noise loud enough to shatter ear-drums.

He had found himself on the ground with fragments of late-Thatcher-era speculative property development cascading down around him. As he staggered to his feet amid the dust he saw one of the black teenagers on the ground sobbing, another cowering over her, and the third – the one who had scowled at him – flat on her back with her lower legs pinned under rubble.

The glass roof was coming down. The girl who had been sobbing on the ground started screaming.

'Pull her out into the street,' he shouted to the crouching girl, who seemed unhurt.

'Yes, do it Beatrice,' called the third girl, twisting herself to sit up. He saw that her left foot was wedged under an orange-painted plywood board representing the side of a sliced melon – part of an India promotional display that had been attached to a cross-beam – and that what looked like tons of rubble was pressing down on the board, threatening at any moment to snap it and bury the girl's foot entirely. Burglar alarms were shrilling to left and right, drowning out the strains of 'You'll Come Back for Me,' that, incongruously, were still twanging from the speakers of the music system, and the acridity of the dust in his nostrils was becoming sharper. Only it wasn't dust at all, it was smoke. Twenty yards beyond the trapped girl he could see flames.

He began clawing at the rubble with his bare hands, hefting planks the way one tosses cabers, heaving and tugging at a long baulk which started off an avalanche that fell away from the girl but half engulfed him. There was another explosion: a blast of heat visible like a golden-tinted phantom – a special effect perhaps from the movie *Ghostbusters IV* – rushed through the precinct, bowling him over, but he was on his feet again in an instant.

'Your beard's burning!' she shouted. 'You've got to go, don't get yourself killed.' He ignored her, continued hefting. 'Please,' she said, in almost a normal voice. 'You've done enough, honest.' He still ignored her. With sudden inspiration she called out, 'Look, my foot's coming free,' and jerked her leg, and he had to hurl himself bodily at the pile of rubble to stop it capsizing on her.

The next thing he remembered was firemen dodging in and out of the smoke like jack-in-a-boxes, but they were too busy with their hoses and the sprouting flames to give him assistance. He had started telling the girl jokes as he leaned across her to get at the pyramid of masonry that held her down, and, even stranger, she had started laughing at them. Some business about her telephone number, and about her lying there while he did all the work, and how they were like Humphrey Bogart and Lauren Bacall (whom she professed never to have heard of). In the strangely tinted gloom – sunlight diluted by smoke – he had been just able to see the white of her teeth as she laughed and the white of her eyes as she gazed up at him. It had helped keep him going. In the end he had shifted what seemed like the entire gable end of the shopping precinct off her foot with his bare bleeding hands, and had carried her out into a street full of fire-engines with blue lights revolving and flashing in the late afternoon sunlight, and behind them ambulances and police cars and policemen and striped tapes across the pavement cordoning all the excitement off from a distant crowd.

'Here, let me – ' said a smoke-goggled paramedic.

'It's all right,' said the girl, 'I can walk.' She slipped out of his arms, stumbling for a moment against his shoulder. 'Look at his hands.'

'His hands,' someone repeated, on a rising note. Officious persons in a variety of uniforms had him by the elbows, steering him away from the girl towards the nearest ambulance. He turned for a last glimpse of her, and was facing the entrance of Dalston Cross when the biggest explosion yet spewed out across the street in a vast yellow gob containing at least one spreadeagled windmilling fireman among the shards and bricks and panels and planks and pieces of paper and bits of window frame. He saw Imogen's face, half-turned towards the blast, take on a momentary golden highlighting in the spurting flames.

And next day she had visited him in hospital, told him that her name was Imogen Campbell, told him that he had left a bloody hand-print on the seat of her brand-new white whipcord slacks, told him, since he lived on his own and had no one to look after him while his hands were bandaged, that he could come and stay for a bit with her family.

She was the first black girl he had ever kissed, clutched, clinched, caressed, cuddled, canoodled with, got clouted by, nipped, nibbled, nuzzled, kneaded, nipple-twiddled, kneeled astride, de-knickered (in spite of bandaged hands), fumbled, frotted, felt up, fingered and, finally, fucked. Only her heels were jaundice-pale, as if she and her clan had been stood one by one on a draining-board and been daubed by God with chocolate sauce from the crown down. Her prominent Staffordshire bull-terrier eyes, with their implausibly long, thick lashes curling in a semi-circle, and the forward tilt of her profile, and her perfect trapezoid nose, like an inverted kite from the front view, had their own peculiar logic which combined with the fact of her blackness to make the faces of white women seem botched and unfinished by comparison. The straight black vertically aligned hairs at the side of her face just in front of her ears were a reminder of his own first

23

attempts at growing sideburns when he was fourteen.

She had been in her school netball team, till dropped for cutting practice. She had biceps that came up like a boy's when she bent her arm, and walked bandy-legged from the crutch, which accentuated the pertness of her bottom. 'You're my Bum of the Year Girl,' he had told her once. 'You're not allowed to call me that,' she had said: *you're not allowed to* was a favourite phrase of hers, usually delivered in a tone of intense solemnity that would dissolve into giggling attempts to keep a straight face.

It was not just her bum either: glimpsing her in the mirror behind a bar, he would be haunted by the unvoiceable fear that one day the *Sun* would start using coloured models and that she would be their first Afro-Caribbean Page Three Girl.

Love is something two people make together.

Their eight months, two weeks and three days together had been the single most important fact of his life during all those four years in jail.

And for most of those four years she had been dead.

Dead. But not cremated, not buried, not given quiet rest in a grave among other graves, in the fields where she had been a child, but dead walking around, dead with strange chemistries going on behind the light in her eyes.

Perhaps at that very moment she was leaning

back laughing out loud, looking into someone's eyes: Imogen's eyes looking out on someone else's world.

He tried to tell himself that the Imogen he had lived with was completely dead, but he couldn't help thinking all the time that in reality what was dead was only part of her. Only her brain was dead. Most of her was as alive as he remembered her: her dark chocolate eyes which he used to pretend were like the eyes on his first teddy-bear but which were actually nothing like, the little chip on her front tooth, the hand that had reached for his on the back seat of the bus, coming home from the hospital the day they took his bandages off, and her firm, insistent fingers. They were still there.

Perhaps it was not all of Imogen that had died. Other parts of Imogen, other people's Imogen, perhaps Imogen's Imogen. Were dead. But not his Imogen.

Not the Imogen all the other Imogens had been inside.

Not the line of her rib-cage standing out above her sucked-in belly as she shucked off her jersey, not her skinny brown shoulder-blades like budding wings or the trackway of little hairs criss-crossing like Anglo-Saxon garters running down from her tummy button to the vee of her unzipped jeans.

She was still there, that Imogen, still alive.

'The Professor', in jail, reckoned there were forty

or fifty artificials by now: the longer-established ones working as scientists alongside human scientists, and the newer ones – like Imogen – living like guinea pigs in a vast obscene programme of biochemical and pharmaceutical experiments: most of them black, because the bodies of black people seemed to age more slowly.

'The Professor' had even told him where the Calloway Institute was.

And Imogen was still there, still alive.

All that was left of Imogen.

VI

He lay awake all night, listening to the wind howling outside. In the morning there were some front gardens with snow-drifts coming up to the first-floor windows.

*

Man reserved his bitterest enmity, and a type of false, sadistic admiration, for those animal species which were the greatest challenge to man's self-image as the master of Nature: the wolf, the elephant, the lion, the tiger. At first man had taken them for symbols of power, and wore their skins as proof of royalty. But all of these creatures were slowly hunted back, penned in, sentenced to slow extinction.

And there was one category of animal, immeasurably stronger and more cunning than the rest, for whom man felt a unique fascination and a unique hatred. So great was this hatred that many nations built fleets of ships designed specially for hunting these prodigious beasts, ships which by the twentieth century were routinely equipped with cannon firing 160-pound harpoons with explosive war-heads. Their prey was not only the biggest being on Earth, it was also, after man himself, the most intelligent.

Some said it was more intelligent.

The whale.

*

Centuries ago seafarers perceived that the muezzin-like cries of the right whale and the rorqual had all the complex rhythms of human conversation, but the stupendous size of these leviathans made close observation impossible.

At last man's technology enabled him to capture and study the smallest of the commoner whales, the dolphin. Within a few years a kind of mythology had grown up about the intelligence and responsiveness of dolphins, and there was even talk of training them so that they could be used by policemen.

Then the first captive killer whales began to be studied. Rarer and larger than the dolphin, they were more difficult to capture and keep in aquaria and were therefore much less accessible to scientific study.

The ability of the dolphin to learn tricks and experimental roles had delighted scientists. But the killer whale learnt even more readily, and apparently for the sheer joy of learning.

It was not often that humans had the chance to watch killer whales in their natural environment attacking other whales, but what reports there were indicated that killer whale packs attacked with a ballet-like skill and co-ordination not found elsewhere in Nature.

Most species of whale have poor eyesight, but their auditory range is six times greater than that of man and they rely on hearing and echolocation for most of their perception of what surrounds them. Like other whale species, the killer whale uses echo location; but it also has keener eyesight than a wolf.

The killer whale is more highly endowed than the smaller dolphin, and equally, the sperm whale is superior to the smaller killer whale. But man has never been able to study the sperm whale under test conditions. An adult bull sperm whale may be sixty feet long, weigh over fifty tons. A man-made aquarium could not house such a colossus.

Though of course they breathe on the surface, sperm whales hunt in the twilight of the ocean depths. Using echolocation they attack giant squids up to a hundred feet long, snatching at the huge invertebrates with mouths that consist of a toothless upper jaw and a lower jaw like a long narrow trap-door edged with two parallel rows of eight-inch, six-pound teeth, and gulping them down whole.

The other large whales dive only to about a hundred metres. Even the superlative killer whale can submerge for only twenty minutes or so. But sperm whales regularly submerge for over an hour, plunging more than a kilometre below the surface.

The sperm whale's brain, the largest known terrestrial brain, is more than five times heavier than that of a human being.

For a long time it was a mystery, what the sperm whales did hundreds of fathoms below the waves, during their long sojourns out of sight of the moon.

VII

The Calloway Institute was a fifteen-foot-high wire fence, a gateway guarded by police, a hint of distant electric lights behind snow-covered trees.

There were Beales-Thomas closed-circuit TV cameras on the fence posts but they were of little use in the steadily falling snow.

Perhaps there were dogs too, but he did not see any as he stumbled across the waist-deep meadow of virgin snow between the fence and the outer*

had expected that, inside the Institute, the staff would be wearing white coats and carrying perspex

* Editor's note: at this point there is a page missing from the original manuscript.

identification cards with their photographs and computer code numbers. But all the people he saw were dressed in casual clothes. The doors in the brightly lit corridors were numbered. One or two were open as he passed; inside he glimpsed rooms like ordinary commercial offices. Every fifty feet along the corridors were maps of the complex with green arrows indicating You Are Here. The maps showed the top two floors as residential quarters.

Nobody paid any attention to him, and though he looked hard at the women, in case one should be Imogen, he managed to avoid meeting anyone's eye. At first he supposed that everyone he passed was a technician or a scientist. But nearly everyone was too young and too athletic-looking – more so than one would have expected in a laboratory – and too many of them were black. Another thing: most of them were on their own, and those in pairs scarcely spoke to one another; they looked perfectly normal, but there was something odd about so many young people going about with so little interaction. Only a young man in a wheel-chair, with a bandaged head, looked as if he might have been involved in brain surgery, yet he seemed no more of a zombie than any of the others. He still had not quite faced up to the recognition that all these people had prosthetic brains when he saw Imogen.

Recognising her despite her bushy Afro hairdo, he quickly dodged down a corridor to escape her, absurdly afraid she would recognise him. Afraid, too, that the pain of seeing her again would be so obvious that it would give him away.

She was wearing jeans, a blue and white sweater. She was on her own, looking fit, full-cheeked, a little preoccupied. She did not glance his way and he was glad he could not see her face properly. He dreaded the moment he would have to look into her eyes, dreaded what he would see there.

He followed her as she ascended a flight of stairs. Those long determined legs, the only legs he had ever wanted to lie between. She turned down a corridor, entered a room.

He saw that they were now in the residential quarters. Imogen had gone into her room. Imogen was alone in her room.

VIII

While the onslaughts of man caused even the whale to dwindle, one great order of animals flourished. Even by the year 2000 there were still at least ten million insects on Earth for every human being: 60,000,000,000,000,000 insects: more than twelve tons of insect for every man, woman and child. There are about 5,000 species of mammal in the world, but over five million different species of insect: as far as is known, none has ever been made extinct by man.

And among all the insects that flew, and the insects that crawled to the end of long leaves, and the insects that swam like tiny clockwork toys, there were species which lived in societies of towering complexity and proliferating restlessness: as complex and restless as the society made by man.

Restless: but unchanging. Compared to humans, the

ants suffered from a degree of rigidity. Man was a new species: perhaps 150,000 years old in his present form. Today's 15,000 species of ant had established their present form 40,000,000 years ago. Their civilisation was not the overnight flowering of corporate fantasies and neurotic enthusiasms, but the meticulous compilation of the wisdom of the aeons. Perfected and refined 400,000 centuries ago, their ways of life had long passed onwards their own infallible logic and their own routines. Continents had risen out of the waters and again sunk, the seasons had altered their cycle, but the ants had marched on like policemen, serene in their teeming thousands of millions, without necessity of change. It would not have been surprising if they had scarcely noticed the existence of the human race, for man's great assault on Nature, and the exponential growth in his numbers, was barely two hundred years old: two centuries against the certain course of uncountable millennia.

Epochs before man's first primate ancestors grubbed for roots in the primeval forests, the ants had established the technique of enslaving lower species. Some species had become entirely dependent on slaves. For thousands of centuries the amazon ant, *Polyergus*, has been unable to gather food or even to feed itself, and has lived by raiding the nests of other ant species to seize larvae, pupae and young adults: slaves to be trained to gather food and cram it into the clumsy mouths of the worker amazons and their amazon queen. Geological eras before man began to improve the strain of his cereal grasses, ants had harnessed the secrets of genetic selection and biochemical engineering and were able to breed specialised fungi which some species still cultivate in their nests today. Dogs were domesticated 12,000 years ago, and a dog will revert to a wild state in a few months: millions of years before the first dog barked, the higher forms of ant began to support spiders and beetles, myrmecophiles or 'ant guests', and 5,000 different species of such pets have evolved which cannot survive unless fed by their ant hosts.

Man had changed so much and so rapidly he had lost sight of how he was changing. He lived between two infinities, the past and the future. But for ants it was the present that was infinite, and they carried on as they had done almost for eternity, and with a relentless certainty.

*

Whales are gourmets of sensual experience in all its variations but ants are simply Awareness. Some species are blind: those species which can see have neither definition of outline nor sense of distance. And no red: they can see colours beyond violet but not red. Their hearing consists only of the sensitivity of their antennae to air movements; the same organ provides them with their sense of touch and taste, and their incredibly acute sense of smell. Strictly speaking all they are aware of is touch, flavoured with an infinity of different odours.

Yet they communicate rapidly. They perform concerted actions evidently purposed well in advance of expected necessities. In the Arabian desert, man may know that rain is coming because enormous numbers of ants that are normally invisible underground can suddenly be seen moving in files on the surface, gathering material to repair the upper galleries of their tunnel cities against the coming deluge. Columns of driver ants have been known to co-operate in food-gathering forays several days' march apart, though human scientists have never managed to identify the location of the directing intelligence.

The ant colony is much more of a biological unit than any human society. It is born and dies with its queen. The queen's death means the death of the colony, though the workers will continue to tend her dead body till it dissolves into dried-out fragments. Some of the higher ants have successive generations of queens inside the same colony, and the hugeness of such a colony will enable it to survive almost indefinitely, but even here the life of the colony revolves around and depends on the queens.

The life of the ant male varies with the species. Some share the appearance and life-style of their sterile worker sisters. Others barely emerge from their pupae and mate immediately with their young queen sisters amid the debris of the hatching chamber. But in most species the males seem to experience life-careers similar to those of the males of the related bee and wasp families: to be fussily nurtured till the day of the mating flight, and thereafter to be left to starve and die.

In some species of ant however it was noted that the numerous males were respectfully tended by the workers even after the mating flight: yet in the highly specialised world of the ant colony they appeared to perform no productive role.

The queens were simply, once the nest was established, egg-laying machines: they might live as long as fifteen years, laying an egg every ten minutes.

The workers, whether or not specialised in their roles, were concerned simply to gather food, tend the helpless queens, males and young, and clean and defend the nest. By means that are still mysterious they communicated with one another, but only on the immediate issues of food and communal defence.

The males could not even find food for themselves, but they could communicate.

The human brain is composed of millions of cells, which together form a single organ within a single biological being.

The male ants within a colony were separate biological beings, though genetically almost identical, but they too could function as a single organ, their rudimentary brains together making up a larger consciousness.

Together, unable even to find their own food, they constituted an intelligence which could make plans and ponder decisions. And communicate with their worker sisters.

IX

She glanced up from her book, her expression curious and alert, but somehow not alarmed.

As their eyes met he felt a chilling wrench in his chest. It really was Imogen sitting there facing him. Somehow he had not quite believed it till that moment: the monstrous enchantments of the laboratory had brought her back to life.

But he knew he must take control, organise the situation, act the policeman.

And as he closed the door softly behind him, and glanced towards the window to check that the curtains were drawn, he asked:

'Do you know who I am? Have you seen me before?'

The Imogen thing stared at him gravely.

Her face was shockingly, heart-turningly exactly as he remembered it, though given an additional, unexpected, intellectual quality by the Afro she wore bushing out at the sides and back: the surrounding black woolliness seemed to emphasise the neat precision of her features. Imogen – the real Imogen – the *dead* Imogen – had had straightened hair arranged in kiss-curls, or ringlets, or in a pony-tail, or tied up in a bun like a twelve-year-old Sikh's – and had always said an Afro was only any use for picking up fluff. Along with the change of hair-do there was a change of manner. The *thing* which now sat staring back at him had a slow-reflexed observant stillness about it, a taking-stock sort of attentiveness, quite unlike the old Imogen's sassy spontaneity: yet there was nothing about its stillness and lack of response that was in any way inhuman.

And then it spoke.

'You are not an artificial,' it/she said. 'But not one of the technical staff either.'

The voice was not Imogen's: the same key, the accent and intonation new.

'You don't seem afraid of me.'

She smiled: not Imogen's smile, a quite different one, lopsided and boyish, shockingly appealing.

'Artificials do not experience fear.'

Once that sudden shocking grin had faded, her face was expressionless. She was wearing a blue and white striped sweater, a silk scarf, factory-faded jeans.

41

No jewellery. Imogen had always worn a ring her grandmother had given her, on the middle finger of her left hand, and often earrings. He could see the tiny pierce marks that still showed on her ear lobes.

He said:

'I used to be the boyfriend of the woman whose body you now occupy.'

There was a long silence between them. The *thing* stared at him. Its eyelids with Imogen's long curling lashes seemed to move quite naturally: it even blinked. The book it had been reading, still in its lap, was by Sartre. The title was appropriate: *Being and Nothingness*.

'I did not choose to be created,' the thing said at last. 'And I did not choose the body which I have been created in. If you feel bitter or angry, don't feel bitter or angry at me. Other people chose to make me, and in this body. But don't think, because this body was only given to me, that this is still the body of your friend. It has been mine for more than three years. It has become me.'

She looked at him, round-eyed, earnest, searching for words.

'Bodies do not remember,' she said. '*Brains* remember. This body does not remember you. And this brain has never seen you before.'

But as she spoke *his* body remembered. Along with

42

his revulsion for this thing not human, and surprised loathing at the physical survival, he was unable to suppress his eagerness to touch and be touched.

'Do you never think of her? The girl whose body you have taken?'

'Not taken: been given. No. I can't feel any special involvement with your friend simply because I now have her body.'

She looked down, perhaps less to avoid his accusing eyes than to gaze at herself.

'We have no emotions as you know them,' she said. 'We learn what we know about emotions from books. From Freud and Klein and R.D. Laing. Perhaps it is all wrong, what we learn.'

'You have no emotions at all?'

'Emotions come from a long symbiosis of mind and body growing up together.' She was looking at him with that almost human earnestness. 'I have your friend's body and a mind constructed in a laboratory. The mind is not a person: we can never be real human beings.'

But as she said this there came to him a feeling of terror – *her* terror – and a need for help.

This was the first feeling he got from her: her fear of not being a person.

X

There is a kind of instability in the human species. We see it in the tendency of all human institutions to degenerate and decay. Because of this instability no human group can survive merely by remaining precisely as it is: it will always suppose itself to be in decline if it does not increase its size, power and complexity. As St Augustine wrote, empires grow through fear of diminution.

This restlessness for growth led first of all to centuries of political conflict between humans. Only ants and men wage war on their own kind. At first the conflicts were tribal and became in turn dynastic, class-based, nationalistic; then ideological: and, at last, racial. Each new mode of conflict incorporated still-vigorous elements of earlier modes; hatred was superimposed on hatred, in geological layers.

In the midst of these centuries of civil war, during the class and nation phases (sometimes called the *democratic* phase), humans also began a massive assault on their physical environment, starting with the obstacles to the unlimited *numerical* growth of their species.

And in Germany, at the cusp of the national and ideological phases, the police pioneered the deliberate, planned, timetabled extermination of an entire race or species. They called it *Die Endlösung*, the Final Solution.

XI

'Have you ever thought of living outside?' he asked.

'Living outside?' she said. 'There would be problems.'

The readiness with which she outlined the problems showed that she had already thought of them several times.

'First, it wouldn't be permitted. They would send police after us. Second, we might be dangerous and disruptive outside. Our brains grow, and can develop almost unlimited mental potential; *they* could never trust us if we were on our own, unsupervised. Third, we couldn't do it on our own. We know the world only from books. To begin with we would be lost, vulnerable, perhaps the more dangerous. We could only survive outside if we had protectors; and what good motive could anyone have for protecting a creature like myself?'

He knew nothing of motives, only that he wanted. He did not even know what it was he wanted. He said:

'I'd like to try.'

She glanced away from him, like a human girl covering a momentary embarrassment, and the quick movement of her head flicked her great bush of hair across her face in a kind of circular swirl. Another quick movement of her head settled her hair back where it had been and she looked at him again.

'Did your friend mean so much to you?'

He did not answer.

He forced himself to try to visualise the laboratory-built abomination behind those eyes: he had only a mental image of a kind of sterile fungus, seething and erupting, but it would not connect itself with the girl he saw in front of him, who asked:

'Did she mean so much to you that you wish to be reminded of her every day by something that is *not* her, never can be her, but only *looks* like her?'

'I think so.'

She smiled. Her smile was frank, enquiring, un-afraid, not now so lopsided. But it was not Imogen's smile.

'I *want* to live outside. I *need* the help of someone like you. I want to find out who I am. If I am a *who*. I want to be part of what's going on. I *want* to be free.'

'There's no such thing as freedom,' he said.

He knew that people's very notion of freedom, and the whole card-castle of their values, belonged wholly to the age and culture into which they chanced to be born, that the opportunities that welcome and the obstacles that oppose are special to each particular age, that people are not themselves but what their times have made them.

But this creature, this she/it, did not belong as ordinary people belonged. Perhaps for her there *was* a possibility of freedom.

'I *need* the help of someone like you,' she said again. 'Perhaps that's why you came.'

He remembered reading somewhere: no-one knows who he is, nor what he has come into the world to do.

*

By the time they reached the toilets he realised that she/it was enjoying the melodrama, the sneaking along corridors, the waiting in doorways, the ducking behind corners out of the way of approaching footsteps. When she walked ahead of him he kept noticing her distinctive leaning-backwards posture, the way her shoulders seemed to go straight while her buttocks corkscrewed slightly. He was sure the real Imogen hadn't walked quite like that, and for a moment he was angry because he couldn't remember precisely how she *had* walked.

In the toilets he explained about the drain-pipe outside.

'Oh I think I can manage that,' the creature declared, smiling almost greedily.

She could too. He went first and waited nervously in the moonlight, at the foot of the drain-pipe: waited in case the creature fell; but she came down with a graceful agility that gave him a strange pang. Seeing him staring up at her anxiously she grinned reassuringly. She jumped the last few feet, landing close beside him, her bush of hair bouncing, in the moonlit snow. Without quite knowing why, he reached out for her.

'Don't,' she said, raising her elbows in a brushing-off gesture. She was still grinning, but for a moment he had a sense of something timid and withdrawing about her.

He thought of Imogen and again he could taste the anger in his throat.

Ten minutes later they were out in the street.

'Thanks,' said the creature. 'That's the most fun I've ever had.'

He felt the same mixing of wonder and anticlimax

that he used to have when a real girl said something that should have been important: and it was only now, in the moonlight, that he noticed that they had given her a different left eyeball.

XII

Originally, human society reproduced the oppressions of the animal kingdom. Just as among animals – insects as well as mammals – a carnivorous minority lived off a majority that subsisted on a mainly vegetable diet, so among humans, from the Neolithic period onwards, a minority of largely meat-eating warriors lived off a majority of largely vegetarian tillers of the soil.

This oppression was as instinctive as the oppression of animal herbivores by animal carnivores. A man born into a warrior caste could no more live like a peasant than a wolf could graze like a sheep. And since, to justify the workings of human nature, man had created God in his own image, social inequality was spoken of as having been ordained by God.

About two hundred years ago man began a decisive

turning away from the age-old model of an aristocracy exploiting and policing an agricultural majority. Machinery created new forms of wealth: a primitive, half-comprehended agricultural science vastly increased the yield of crops. The tillers of the soil ceased to comprise the majority of the population. Soon most people in advanced societies had nothing at all to do directly with the creation of any visible form of consumable, whether agricultural or industrial. Yet as human civilisation freed itself from its resemblance to animal society, man himself did not become free.

Man had liberated himself from the crudities of the food chain, but had enslaved himself to the machine, to bureaucracy which was the organisational and intellectual counterpart of the machine, to social theories which were modelled on the machine, to materialism which was the religion of the machine, to the city which was a machine in which man could live in large groups.

The Machine liberated man from Nature: the Machine was the enemy of Nature, an embodied ideology of non-Life.

It was at this stage of human history that the long war against the animals, the most vital embodiment of Nature, became a war of extermination.

The past is the womb of the future. We can no more

hope to escape from the destiny we inherit than we can expect an animal of one species to give birth to an animal of another.

XIII

They lived on the second floor of a house in Finsbury Park, at the top of a flight of narrow creaking stairs with half the banisters missing.

The windows were almost permanently cobwebbed over with frost. Slush kicked off shoes in the hallway in the evening would still be lying in gobbets on the door-mat the following morning.

Outside the snow flitted down as insistently as the ticking of a clock. Tarts stood at street corners in twos and threes, defying the unspeakable cold and the snowflakes which chased each other in flocks over the pavement. The police had better things to do these days and no longer harassed the street girls. But the high price of petrol had put an end to kerb-crawling, and there were fewer foreign seamen and travelling salesmen. Nature had stretched out its great hand, and civilisation was beginning to close down. Everyone was staying home, staying close, burying themselves amid the snow-covered spoil-heaps of Victorian urbanisation, adjusting to the realities of living in the tomb of hope: and the tarts talked mainly to one another.

There was a flattened-out cat in the ice at the crossing at the end of the block. Each day the outline of the unrecognisable yukkinesses squashed out of its still-recognisable mouth seemed to change shape in the ice, as if with a changing message.

The traffic on the main road consisted mainly of police vans with flashing blue lights: there were only a few overcrowded buses and a handful of private cars to be seen now. But people had become inured to the cold, and when it was not snowing too heavily the pavements outside the pubs were crowded with lounging, watching drinkers. Occasionally there would be outbreaks of shouting: in the morning the hard-trodden snow on the pavement would often be dappled with spots of blood: probably only a broken nose, but who knows? Possibly a knife wound, the victim whisked away, wrapped in polythene sheeting, left in a cellar somewhere. Regularly on Saturday nights the shop fronts and the heaps of snow would be lit up by the flash of paraffin bombs. Paraffin, not petrol: petrol was now hard to find. The flames would die down after a few minutes, not hot enough to leave more than a smear of black. The police usually didn't even bother to phone the fire brigade.

Imogen accepted it. There was no point in his explaining that not everyone lived like this: it was more and more the case that everyone did.

He thought of summer while outside the snow fell solemnly: thought of summer evenings in the times before perpetual winter, with the other Imogen, Imogen in jeans and sleeveless T-shirt, looking out over the wheatfields of southern Essex in the brightness of an evening at the moment when the quality of the light changed, while the sound of 'You'll Come Back for Me' came from the car radio behind them.

Now he was alone in alien London, trapped in perpetual winter with this ice-cold imitation Imogen who had been put together in a laboratory, living their private nightmare in the suburbs of a world dying of its own paranoia.

He taught her to cook, fed her, sometimes brought her breakfast in bed. He gazed at her gooseberry-fuzzed arms in her sleeveless nightshirt; and sometimes she let him stroke them. And as she sat up, leaned forward over her breakfast tray, he could see down her open V-neck, see the caramel inner slopes of her breasts curving almost but not quite as far as the half-remembered mocha rosettes at their tips, and he would wonder what Golem's consciousness, in cancerous whorls and lobes, swelled and proliferated at the back of her calm eyes.

The new left eye they had given her was almost a perfect match with the other, perhaps a fraction less darker-edged around the pupil, and with other minute, indefinable variations which in some lights gave her an attractively squinty expression. It gave her twenty-twenty vision: the old Imogen had been short-sighted in that eye.

He asked if they had changed any other of her organs.

'No. Except for my brain everything else is exactly the way it was Before.'

She read a lot. The TV no longer worked: the static on the screen was like one of the blizzards outside: up and down both sides of every street the TV aerials were thickened by ice into the semblance of a host of abandoned skeletons, manning the topmost ramparts of the frozen city. So she read: books from the public library on history and sociology and psychology and, most of all, philosophy. As she stared down at the pages her face would take on an intent, astute look that reminded him of the coffin mask of an Egyptian queen he had once seen in the British Museum. And the water in the pipes sang to her in the evenings, telling her that they too were not frozen by the colder-than-a-refrigerator cold.

Often she didn't talk much. Answered questions briefly and to the point:

'What would you like to do tonight?' – 'Read this book.'

'What's it about?' – 'Philosophy. It's Descartes. He's the man who refuted the proposition that it was impossible to be certain – '

(And there was a bit more that sounded much the same to him.)

'Are you happy?' – 'I'm all right. I feel OK.'

'Are you glad you came away with me?' – 'Yes.'

'Don't you ever wonder what I'm thinking about?' – 'No. But you can tell me if you like.'

And she would look across at him encouragingly, those alert eyes searching his face. He really could tell her what he was thinking about: if he wanted to. But when he didn't say anything for two minutes, she would squirm herself a little deeper into her armchair and continue reading.

He found a copy of *Undine*, the story of a water fairy who could only acquire a soul by living in love with an ordinary mortal, but her only remark on reading it was, 'So they had people like me even before the Calloway Institute.'

Her occasional demands for information – How

many people believe in the Bible? – Where do they take the rubbish after the dustbins have been emptied? – Which bit of the taste of water is the fluoride? – Why do people become policemen? – would take him by surprise, forcing her on his attention like a small demanding child.

In some ways she seemed very young, very unself-conscious. She liked plonking her feet in puddles of slush, catching at snow-flakes with her tongue, climbing fences, throwing snowballs, making paper darts. She had a little girl's trick of scratching the back of her calf when it itched with the shin of the other leg, and when coming downstairs on the bus would always jump the last two steps with her feet together.

She liked salty foods, cold sausages, Marmite.

She hated men looking at her. Especially she hated *him* looking at her.

'What are you looking at?' she asked angrily. 'I'm not bits. I'm me.'

And yet, when their open fire had got their living room warm enough for her to take off her pull-over, and she noticed him glancing at her arms, she would show them off to him proudly, even let him touch.

She had biceps that came up like a boy's when she bent her arm.

'You keep looking at me as if you were going to have me for dinner,' she said once.

He was just in the act of dishing up their meal, lamb stew, chunks of lamb with the bone in it, and suddenly he thought, this is what stew made of human limbs would look like. And he thought of the surgeons' scalpels cutting into Imogen, wondered what they had done with the paste of scrambled brains they had scooped from her – the real Imogen's – head.

He did not know how to respond to the creature he was living with.

He could not pretend she was Imogen. More and more she did not even remind him of Imogen.

The subject of Imogen – the *real* Imogen – was of course taboo between them, but they often discussed her – the *new* Imogen's – predicament. They referred to it as Her Problem. They talked about it, but still he felt dissatisfied, obscurely cheated.

But several times a day, something in the way she sat curled in her armchair, her head bent over her book, something in the unembarrassed manner in which she reached into her pullover front to adjust her bra, something in the round-eyed enquiry of her expression as she looked at him, made him think, with an almost physical catching at his breath, *how beautiful she is*.

And the thought buried just below the surface of his

mind, that *she's not real, not even really alive*, would make her beauty wrong, unspeakably vile.

But that thought day by day became weaker.

Every day, something she said, something in one particular gesture or look, announced triumphantly *I'm me, I'm alive, I'm real*.

With power cuts so frequent, people depended on candles and coal fires: beaten down by the new enemies which had risen so unexpectedly, the city was reverting to an earlier technology. And he would look at her face during the power cuts, watch how the planes and angles of her face were highlighted in the candle's glow and stirring as if in tune with the soft ebb and flow of light on the ceiling, and wonder, what was it behind that calm mask? And a shadow in the little hollow at the base of her throat, above the ends of her collar bones, reminded him of how once, in a different lifetime, he had trailed his finger over that throat, stroked upwards to the parted lips, smiled as those white teeth bit playfully at his hand.

And outside the lightning would flicker like strobe lights, throwing the silhouette of the city against a garish sky.

*

On his release from prison the jostle and dissonance of

the streets had been startling but he had been used to it before and it quickly again became familiar. But the shock of those first few hours on the Outside was recent enough for him to know exactly how she felt when, for the very first time, she faced the outside world.

He saw how she cringed at the blind impetuous charging of the few remaining cars, hesitated and drew back at the denser crowds of shoppers. He could see how surprised she was by the litter, the discarded Coke cans, the chocolate-bar wrappers spread on the slushy pavements like the squashed remains of large butter-flies. And when they passed a mother with a young child, he saw how she turned and stared in fascination.

'People seem so angry,' she remarked. 'Even the little children seem angry.'

It was a mistake to keep staring at the children: people were afraid that *they* – the enemies of the human race, whoever they were – knew it would be easier to get at the children first.

But he saw it with her eyes, how everyone gave off a sense of tenseness and hostility, how even standing still they seemed poised to flee or pounce, how everyone emanated a kind of fear. There was something *electric* about people. He had noticed it in his first few hours outside jail. Then he had liked it. He had thought, after the stultifying months behind the bars, that people outside were simply more alive. But now he understood that, in jail, what people showed was, as well as a kind of numbness, the relaxation and calm and certainty that came from acceptance and complete knowledge of the worst; whereas outside they were wound up, strung out, crucified by fear and doubt. They were not more alive, simply more in pain.

And he saw that she knew this, as if instinctively. Because she was not human, she saw how humans lived every moment crucified by fear.

*

They lived like that too. They took it for granted that the police or the officials from the Institute, or both together, would come after them. They lived for each hunted moment and it seemed right that they should be living in a city, in a society, which no longer knew it had a future. It suited him to feel they were living in a world where there would soon be nowhere left to run to.

And yet he could not help wondering about what lay ahead. Somehow her existence, and their living together, had half-persuaded him that there might be such a thing as freedom after all, but he still did not know whether freedom was the ability to predict a future, and design one's own role in that future, or whether freedom was the ability to decide and create the future out of the maze of options which surrounded them.

What he did know was that people were born to live a thousand lives, and die having lived just one.

*

It was almost as if in order to convince himself that she was real that he set out to seduce her.

Because in one sense he already possessed her, he did not want to force her.

He kept thinking of ways he could initiate a habit of physical contact.

He began to grab at her hand when he wanted to draw her attention to things. It was a warm, solid hand. But passive: there was never any answering pressure.

The first time they went to the cinema, he put his arm along the back of the seat. She gave him a look. He sat gazing at her, ignoring the film. She looked at him, smiled and returned her attention to the screen.

He thought he ought not to hurry things.

Next day he brought her breakfast in bed. She was awake and sat up unself-consciously in her nightshirt.

'You're still not bored with breakfast in bed?'

'No. Where's yours?'

He brought his own in and sat on the edge of the bed, using her legs as a rest for his tray. She smiled at this, jogged the tray a little by moving her foot, just to tease him.

She looked like a black Madonna in her nightshirt, her face vulnerable and naked from being newly out of sleep. He asked:

'Can I kiss you?'

'No. I don't want you to kiss me.'

And she looked at him solemnly.

He thought about making love to her. Nose to nose lips to lips tongue to tongue right hand to left breast – she would handle his erection as expertly as a lever, would be wet for him the moment he pressed her nipple, and afterwards would say, 'That was just what I needed.'

That evening in the kitchen, he put his arms round her from behind.

'*Don't*,' she said plaintively; and as he hesitated she moved to break free.

And for a moment she seemed to concentrate a fierce will. Afterwards he found it difficult to describe what it was that happened. A feeling of remoteness and emptiness and helplessness and physical near-paralysis seemed to hit him like an electric shock. It was as if his whole being, mental and spiritual as well as physical, was being held together by strings, and they had all been cut at once. He sank into the nearest chair. She stood in front of him, smiling with sympathetic attention.

Then it was over.

'You've made me forget what we were cooking,' she said with a sweet moue. 'Do you remember?'

'Yes, of course, macaroni cheese with olives and mango slices,' he said without meaning to, though the idea seemed immediately familiar, as if he had had it four minutes previously and briefly forgotten it. He stood up and took a packet of macaroni from the cupboard.

She followed his every move as he cooked with wondering concentration, like a devoted pupil, leaning over his shoulder now and then, handing him things with a rapt teenage smile.

He was obscurely aware that something frightening had happened to him, but he was not frightened. Her mere presence seemed to have a calming, reassuring effect on him. But after that, whenever he thought of making a grab at her, he would immediately afterwards think: *she* wouldn't like it.

*

She spoke quite naturally of *we*. *We* must economise. *We* need a new broom. *We* could go out.

And there was that indefinable sense about the house of its being a shared home.

It was more than the sum of the details of their shared life. More than:

Her long crinkly hairs in the wash-basin.

Her bra and panties swirling around in the washing machine along with his shirts and handkerchiefs.

The book she had been reading on the table, to be moved away when he set the cutlery.

The carton of Tampax in the lavatory and occasionally a piece of toilet paper browned with her faeces floating soddenly in the toilet bowl.

(And once an especially intimate vision of a ten-inch turd which she had failed to flush away at the first go.)

But he was sharing his life with *what*?

He was constantly looking for her to behave just like a *real* girl, but more than their living together, what made them most a couple was their shared secret knowledge of the truth about her, and the way they could talk about it.

*

But of course they did things together. Went out side by side.

She did not like pubs. She liked pinball and space

invaders machines, and she tried smoking cigarettes, but she said:

'There's too many people. And every time I look round there's a man staring at me.'

'Which man?'

'Not the same one, stupid. It's just that whichever way I look there's bound to be some man eyeing me up. The way people relate to one another always seems out of sync. When you're interested you pay too much attention, when you're not interested you pay too little.'

'Do *I* pay too much attention?'

'Far too much. You make me feel sometimes I'm still in a laboratory – but the wrong one. Don't worry, though, I know it's part of the deal.'

(He was beginning to understand that, for her, the *newness* of her body, and his not-so-new interest in it, and his presence reminding her of her body's previous existence, caused her to be fascinated, obsessed, insatiably curious – but afraid – of her own body. That was why she hated being stared at.)

*

He took her to a disco, but only once.

She looked around at the other people.

'I like the way they dress,' she said.

She didn't think much of the music but she liked looking at the people. After a while she agreed to dance. She got the hang of it very quickly – she learnt *everything* phenomenally quickly – but when there was a slow number and he put his arms around her she said:

'You know I don't like that. I'd rather sit down.'

The record they were playing was 'You'll Come Back for Me'.

While he was at the bar buying more drinks a man tried to pick her up. When he approached with their drinks a black youth with wire-rimmed glasses and spots and hair done all round in short thick braids like sooty catkins was standing beside her. She was speaking to him, responding to questions. She seemed composed and turned with a smile as he came up beside her with their drinks. A real 'Here's my male with my Pepsi' smile, he thought with a now familiar pang. He wondered how she would react if he told the man with the braids to piss off and find his own.

The man noticed his approach and grinned derisively, as if to say, *Don't envy you your share of the world's twat, mate.* 'Well, see you around,' he said, and melted into the crowd.

'Was he trying to pick me up?' she asked.

'What do *you* think?'

'Do you suppose he could feel the hostility eman-ating from you?' She sipped from her glass. 'I swear you've changed all the ion particles in my drink from positive to negative.'

She was beginning to make jokes like that: it was the nearest she came to paying him a compliment.

*

Some days she was depressed.

'I just feel I'm nothing,' she said. 'I don't know what I'm for or why.'

And once she said:

'I sometimes wish they had never made me. What right had they to *make* me?'

'Real people feel like that sometimes.'

It was the first time he had spoken to her of *real people*, in contradistinction to herself. She did not seem to mind, but said:

'It's different for them. They're real. They belong. I don't even really exist. I'm just part of an experi-ment.'

'You're real to me,' he said.

And when he said it, suddenly it was true.

'But I'm not real to *me*.'

'But you are to *me*,' he insisted. And he took her elbows in his hands and willed her to believe: 'You must be real. If you aren't, how do you explain *my* being here?'

*

He dreamed the strangest dream about the previous Imogen.

She was working the streets in Finsbury Park, a streetwalker not yet losing her looks. It was before the onset of the Unending Winter, and she was still the girl he had glimpsed in mirrors behind bars. One off-duty night Imogen bumped into a woman at the cinema. It seemed to be a replica of herself, but twenty years older, dressed in clothes that belonged to a differently educated personality, with a look in the eye and round the mouth that spoke of a different life. This woman even wore a wedding ring. She looked exactly the way Imogen supposed she might have looked if she had been born into a different family, in a different decade, in a different life.

The fact that this woman was so much older was almost the most unnerving thing about the encounter.

It wasn't Imogen's future self or anything like that: the older woman did not come from the future. She seemed to be the old-fashioned chapel-going type, fond of flowered hats.

In his dream the original Imogen explained all this to him.

Two weeks later she saw the woman again, at Sainsbury's. This time the woman saw her staring and smiled welcomingly.

'Come and have a cup of tea,' she said.

Imogen questioned her frantically. The woman answered all her questions carefully but with an amusement that seemed rehearsed. No, they were not related. Her father was a Mr So-and-So from Kingston or wherever, and her mother had been Miss So-and-So from St Vincent. She patiently listed the maiden names of her two grandmothers and four great-grandmothers . . . Despite an irritating conviction that they were talking at cross-purposes, Imogen felt strangely at ease with her new acquaintance, and when the latter said, 'You must come and meet the others,' she agreed.

Imogen went to an address she had been given in Tottenham. When she rang the bell the door was immediately opened by an elderly woman whom Imogen recognised with terror. It was a replica of herself born in 1915, and now extremely old.

There were eight women there: all black, but of varying shades. They were all of different ages, though there were two in their thirties who were close enough in age to appear identical twins, separated at birth and, very noticeably, fed on different diets; and a school-teacher aged twenty-six who looked like a replica of Imogen *now*, but physically altered by insomnia.

None of them was related to any of the others.

It seemed to be like this, the school-teacher explained to Imogen. There's about six thousand million people alive in the world today. Perhaps fifty thousand million people have lived since the beginning of the human race. Fifty thousand million – fifty milliard, fifty US billion totally unique individuals. Helluva lot of variation, the school-teacher seemed to imply. 'Have you any idea how many people you look at closely enough to recognise afterwards, in the space of a year? Probably a thousand. Say a hundred thousand in an entire lifetime. That means that in a population of two million, if you had an exact double the chances are ten to one against either of you noticing the other, provided you weren't introduced by a third party.'

The group had no idea how many more women existed in the world who were essentially identical to them except in age. They did know, however, that there were other such groups.

It was more than simply amazing. It was strangely moving. Despite the differences of age and background all the women had the kind of rapport which is spoken of in the case of identical twins. They understood one another as soon as they began to speak.

The functioning of all their minds independently yet in unison created a sense of clairvoyance.

But why, the original Imogen had asked, had no-one detected this phenomenon before?

The answer was: they had.

Throughout history there had been ruling dynasties where fathers passed on their royal power not to their sons, but to adopted heirs. In the Roman Empire Nerva adopted Trajan who adopted Hadrian who adopted Pius Antoninus who adopted Marcus Aurelius, who left the imperial power to his real son Commodus, who was the first failure of the family. In Tibet, future Dalai Lamas were identified from among the children of poor Tibetan families. The degree of *physical* resemblance was generally obscured for other people by the differences of age, diet, dress.

The school-teacher also thought the same principle was involved in the recruitment to the military orders of the Middle Ages, such as the Knights Templars and the Knights of the Sword. The Order of Knights Templars had been broken up by an alliance of ecclesiastical and secular authorities, and many of the knights had been executed as magicians. It was already clear to Imogen's group that, when together, their combined brains had enormous potential power. Perhaps there was something of the sort involved in witchcraft covens.

'We could take over the world,' said the young school-teacher.

At this point he woke.

He realised that either no-one else ever in the history of the world had had the same idea as in his dream, or else many people had and they were connected. This made him afraid to tell his dream to the new Imogen.

*

They managed to avoid the subject of the real Imogen till one day she asked:

'Am I *anything* like Imogen?'

He looked at her and thought.

'You *look* like her. And that's all. That's the only similarity.'

The same little chip on one of her front teeth, the same trapezoid nose, the same semi-circle curl to her eye-lashes. The same Bum of the Year Girl body.

And he wondered how it was that there had never been any question of not calling her Imogen.

There was no good reason for not calling her Imogen. There were days when he never even thought about the old Imogen.

XIV

It is a mistake to see the relationship between man and animals as a relationship imposed solely at the initiative of man. Till three hundred years ago, the people of Northern Europe depended on kites to scavenge and clean organic matter from the streets of their cities, but these kites were in no sense tame. Smaller creatures such as earthworms and bees played a vital part in the productive cycle of the soil: bees could be enslaved, but they could never be properly tamed, nor could their innate routines be changed. On balance, man's relationship with domesticated animals contributed much less to his mode of existence than his relationship with the untamed and untameable, the wild birds who scavenged, the invertebrates who haunted the upper soil and lived on and among the plants, the fish who swarmed in the oceans and rivers.

And even before the Struggle began, animals were not everywhere in retreat.

Man had triumphed because of his adaptability, but he was not the only animal able to adapt.

Even in overcrowded Britain animals changed their life styles, made a counter-attack on their dwindling environments.

Not just the house mice who had flourished for centuries as parasites on man, the black rats who established themselves in the twelfth century, the brown rats who joined them in the eighteenth century and soon outnumbered them, and the rabbits and pheasant who also came in the Middle Ages.

Robins started moving into the cities from the shrinking countryside in the eighteenth century. When the robin perched on a garden spade became established as a Christmas card cliché, *Erithacus rubecula* had only recently impinged on man's consciousness with its seeming fondness for human company. Blackbirds and song thrushes followed, became familiar denizens of suburban gardens. Another refugee from the farmlands, the blue tit, learnt to steal milk from bottles on doorsteps within half-a-dozen years of the introduction of the silver-foil milk-bottle top. Starlings began to breed in London in the 1930s. Soon the racket they made settling down to roost had become almost the only sound to be heard on an autumn evening among the deserted streets and office-buildings around the Guildhall and the Bank of England. (They had also emerged as the commonest species of bird in the United States, having been introduced there only in 1890, when a man who wished to establish in North America every species of bird mentioned in Shakespeare released forty pairs in New York's Central Park.) During the 1960s even the kestrel became a city dweller, nesting on the top of tower blocks and police stations, and the wood pigeon began to colonise London's parks alongside the more familiar rock dove. The collared dove, which first arrived in Britain only in 1955, gradually spread everywhere, in country and in town. The herring gull began to become a common city scavenger, doubling its population every six years and pushing out the jackdaw, the species which over three centuries ago helped to drive the kite from its traditional habitat in the stinking streets of medieval English towns.

Roe-deer recolonised twenty English counties after the Second World War. Rabbits, which outnumbered humans in Britain two to one before myxomatosis struck the species, were common again two decades later.

Meanwhile bands of feral mink lurked in the neighbourhood of the fur farms from where their forefathers escaped; in the centre of Leicester miniature deer of Indian origin lived furtive nocturnal lives among the shrubberies of public gardens.

If every man, woman and child in Britain were to die tomorrow the land would not remain empty.

XV

Jobs were difficult to find – even before the Emergency there had been three million unemployed – and they dared not risk the Social Security investigating Imogen's background. But it was necessary to eat, necessary to seek some occupation during the skyless days of waiting sandwiched between long darknesses. They were taken on at London Zoo. Because of the all-pervasive rumours that were never officially denied, people did not like working around animals any more. The zoo could not afford to be choosy about staff and did not make trouble when Imogen said she had forgotten her National Insurance number.

Nobody – no holiday-makers or troops of school children – visited the zoo any more. Especially not the children: everyone was afraid that the animals would somehow try to get at the children first. Every time an animal escaped, even small monkeys, there were scare headlines on the front pages of the newspapers that had managed to appear that day, and discussions on the buses – if they were running – about why the government did not order all the zoo animals to be destroyed.

Shot was the word people liked to use.

Actually, it was a matter of prestige as far as the government was concerned. Despite the Emergency there was a desire to deny the reality of the threat and carry on as if everything was normal: and that included maintaining zoos full of animals. There was the so-called scientific argument too: the purpose of menageries was ultimately scientific, and the human race couldn't possibly allow itself to be stampeded into altering the style of its scientific investigations merely by pressure from a load of beasts, by a threat which hadn't even been officially acknowledged.

But more and more people began to talk about the inmates of zoos as 'our prisoners' or even 'our hostages'. Of course it was acknowledged that *they* did not take prisoners; but it was an assertion of human superiority to conduct the Struggle on *human* principles, rather than copy how *they* behaved.

In fact, because of food shortages and problems with recruiting staff, some of the smaller zoos had closed down, and others had disposed of – gassed rather than shot – their less important specimens, but the principle remained that the zoos were still functioning, still open to the public.

But the public did not come.

London Zoo, when they joined the staff, was like a prison camp. Beyond the frozen labyrinth of Camden Town, coils of barbed wire to a depth of ten yards surrounded the electrified perimeter of Regent's Park. Behind the electrified fence was a fire zone monitored by batteries of photo-electric cells, Beales-Thomas scanners and infra-red detector devices; the watch-towers were equipped with triple .22 Armalite mountings and 0.50 Colt machine guns loaded with a sequence of tracer, explosive and AP bullets. For the elephants. Outside the gate – there was only one gate now – was a lorry pool. There was constant movement: of zoo staff going off in parties for weapons training at the new military depot in St James's Park, of police and army personnel arriving to attend animal-handling courses, of emergency teams speeding off in gas tenders to investigate reported animal sightings. Behind the fire zone things were much quieter: only the zoo staff going around in threes to attend to the feeding and cleaning, and the animals pacing their cages, watching, waiting.

'Poor animals,' said Imogen. 'Because I'm a woman,

descended, part of me, from a 150,000-year-old oppression, I sometimes feel I ought to join up with *them*.'

*

The zoo gave Imogen the second big relationship of her life, with a female orang-utan who made things for her out of twigs, became extraordinarily excited when she picked them up, but had dreadfully coarse manners.

They used to touch fingers like God and Adam on the ceiling of the Sistine Chapel.

The orang had orange coconut-fibre hair and immensely long, black-nailed fingers, and a grey face with pink-lidded eyes. She slept in a tree perch consisting of five or six pieces of wood which she would re-arrange in the evenings and again first thing in the morning, and wait eagerly to show it to Imogen when she arrived for duty. They would stand side by side – tall/slim/black, short/squat/ginger-blonde – as if discussing it, and as if responding to suggestions the orang would dart forward now and then to move a piece of wood here, pull a stick further out there.

Imogen was constantly being warned not to become too familiar with the creature: all the other staff were afraid of it. But when Imogen left for home in the evening the orang would cling to her and whisper in her ear, and sometimes kiss her delicately on the corner of the mouth.

Sometimes, in the mornings, the orang would have hung up banana skins in decorative rows. These would remain until Imogen had looked at them.

If one gave the orang a composite object she would dismantle it without breaking any of the pieces. One could give her a toy made out of Lego, and the box, and she could take the Lego apart and put the pieces in the box, and close it.

Somehow all the animals seemed more intelligent when Imogen was around.

He asked:

'Do you think they're intelligent enough to give names to one another?'

'Yes,' she said. 'And I've sometimes thought the wind was trying to pass me messages, even in a tin can rolling on the ice, and the animals sense it too. They think of me as the "Wind-Female".'

*

He was assigned to the gorilla team. There were four men in his shift, and the others were constantly bitching that the zoo, or the government, was too mean to provide the remote-control handling devices that they needed: 'I mean the *smallest* of them is two hundred kilograms of solid muscle, a single punch from one would buckle your ribs right up against the front of your spine.'

This kind of talk was not unnecessarily alarmist. The gorilla pens were arranged so that the beasts could be confined to one section while the other was being slopped out. One day it was noticed that in one of the pens a twig had been cunningly inserted so as to interfere with the movement of the bolt that secured the door between the sections. If it had not been observed in time, the door could have been thrown open by the gorilla – a seemingly placid elderly male – and the man cleaning out the empty half of the pen might have been beaten to paste.

They were less impressed by the narrowness of the escape than by the simple and elegantly ingenious way the twig had been placed to interfere with the bolt.

There was little possibility that the blocking of the bolt had not been deliberate. Gorillas were much less inquisitive than chimpanzees and showed almost no disposition to fiddle with objects and to explore their possible use. And it had been an *old* gorilla, which for years had done little else but sit around looking immensely dignified and ignoring anything it couldn't eat.

'What I can't understand is why they are so strong

and so clever,' the shift foreman would say, peering at them suspiciously through his horn-rimmed spectacles. He meant that normally gorillas lived on the ground and fed off shrubs, and to feed off shrubs requires only the intelligence of a cow. They did not often climb trees because of their weight, and consequently did not need such strong arms. Though they did not use tools, their thumbs had much greater opposability than those of the chimpanzees and orangs, and they had much greater manipulative ability with small objects. Most animals are only intelligent enough, strong enough and agile enough to handle their own ecological niche: the foreman could not understand why the gorillas were designed for a much more demanding existence than they normally had.

He seemed to be saying: what right has an animal to be so intelligent?

XVI

Because of the cold, the sparrows and pigeons which formerly lived among the house roofs had disappeared. And because of the way people now felt about animals the cats and dogs had gone too, to the RSPCA or to the Animal Centres set up by the police in every district. Humanity seemed to be left in sole possession of the besieged city beyond the zoo.

But one moonlit evening Imogen found a half-frozen blackbird on the window-sill, wedged up against the window pane for warmth. Once indoors it revived, ate cake crumbs, flew about the room, but showed little interest in leaving.

They called it Arnold. It never allowed him to pick it up, though it took bread from his hand, but it seemed to enjoy having Imogen stroke its head with her finger. It would respond to her like a child, sulking, chirping, shrinking away and sidling back if not pursued, simultaneously anxious to obtain and to avoid physical contact. It would sing to her when they came home in the evening, long carols with contralto diapasons and tremolos, carefully organised into paragraphs or canticles punctuated by higher-toned arpeggios and unexpected pauses during which he would watch them out of one fathomless yellow-rimmed eye for a long moment, before launching into the next section. Imogen used to say: 'I expect he's trying to tell us something.' When there was a thunder storm it would perch on the back of her chair by her shoulder and fluff out its feathers after each crash above their heads. It roosted every night on top of the wardrobe in her room.

'I feel just like a real human being,' said Imogen, 'now that I've even got a pet.'

Outside the city lay under a white blanket, as if buried under the souls of all the animals men had killed throughout history.

She read books from the library about the migration of birds – how every year for centuries birds had followed the seasons from land to land, from continent to continent (some, like the Arctic tern, from pole to pole), navigating in vast leaderless flocks, guided by polarised light, using a fan-like structure in their eyeballs for a sextant. Blackbirds belonged to a species that had never used to migrate: but then, as the whole nature of the climate changed in England, they too had flocked together and fled to an unknown land. Arnold was perhaps the last one left.

A couple of times when the weather was briefly a little less glacial than usual they would push up the window to relieve the fug in their rooms and Arnold would perch on the lower sill, looking out and listening, alternately erecting the feathers on his little black head into a kind of crew-cut, and then flattening them. Occasionally an imperceptible stirring in the frozen wilderness outside would attract his attention and he would hop to left or right along the sill to hear better, though all there ever was out there was the dripping of water and the furtive creak of shifting ice.

And one night when they came home from the zoo, he lay dead on the table. His head was doubled up under his breast, and his wings were half spread, so that his corpse on the table-cloth looked like a black W.

*

Afterwards they knew that the black W was a sign, for this phase of their lives came to an end first thing the following morning.

He had just switched on the radio, prior to making

the coffee for breakfast, and was twiddling the knob, trying to escape from a government spokesperson who was pooh-poohing the latest reports of ants in the Internet, when there was a crash and a splintering at the door and the apartment was suddenly full of policemen.

They were carrying pistols.

'Sit down and shut it,' said a young police sergeant in glasses, motioning to the sofa with the barrel of his Browning 9mm.

Another of them drew back the curtains and glared out.

The window was much less frosted-over than usual and outside there was an incredibly kitsch sunrise, all vermilion and magenta. It reminded him of an over-painted tin tray that had been around the house when he was a kid.

Two officers with scanner devices checked the rooms. They were similar to the Beales-Thomas metabolisation detectors used at the zoo, but of a more expensive design.

'Nothing here,' they reported.

The whole thing was so familiar, especially the bitter taste in the mouth and the feeling of helplessness.

Imogen looked around with big frightened eyes at first but then apparently forced herself to relax. When one of the policemen picked up the book she had been reading – Benedetto Croce's *Autobiography* – and made a face, she even smiled a little.

The chief superintendent who seemed to be in charge conferred with someone over his police radio. Then he peered at them over the tops of his bi-focals.

He said: 'You're wanted.'

XVII

In the twilight of a sudden snow-storm it was impossible to make out where they were being driven. Several minutes became confused. They seemed to be going round and round inside one of those old-fashioned Father Christmas paper-weights that you have to shake and turn upside-down, except that, instead of the falling snow becoming less as the moments passed, it seemed to become thicker. Finally, the police-car stopped in a street of tall buildings which hovered like phantoms in the flickering white gloom, and the two of them were ushered through revolving doors.

A lift took them up to the roof, a door was pushed open, and they confronted a number of men in goggles and flying-suits who stood in the scudding snow around a twin-rotored helicopter in Royal Navy livery.

'Good luck,' said the chief superintendent.

'This way!' called one of the goggled airmen, waving them over to a door in the side of the helicopter. As they climbed in, the engines cough-coughed-choked into life and the rotors began to skim round.

'Get strapped in,' the airman shouted, pointing to a pair of seats.

The door closed behind them with the plump square definitive sound of a cell-door closing on a four-year sentence.

They sat down opposite a thin-faced, soldierly-looking gentleman wearing a fur-collared coat and, unexpectedly, a bowler hat and a monocle. One could have imagined flying to a rendezvous with him in the cabin of a lend-lease B-17 Flying Fortress; to encounter him in this plexiglass flying spaceman's helmet of a helicopter was a break with something. They looked at one another without recognition while the crewman helped them with their safety harnesses. When he had finished and gone forwards, the man with the monocle leaned across and said:

'The sound-proofing leaves much to be desired, but I'd better tell you what this is all about.'

*

His name was Garland. He was a brigadier in the

Royal Corps of Signals, assigned to GCHQ (Government Communications Headquarters) at Cheltenham. During the past few years he had been involved in top security areas: electronic surveillance, remote control espionage, monitoring of high-frequency military radio transmissions inside foreign countries. He was in charge of evaluating this kind of material and advising the Cabinet on its political and strategic implications.

His men were of course accustomed to all manner of scrambling devices, code systems and techniques of jamming. About a month previously they had begun to pick up radio transmissions from perfectly familiar sources, scrambled in a completely novel and unexplainable way. There are various devices for disguising voices or other types of signal so that they are unintelligible to anyone without a reception device adjusted correctly to unravel the way the signal has been disguised; but these signals had been scrambled *without* a device. Signals, sometimes encoded messages of secondary military importance and low security rating, sometimes signals from the control towers of civilian aerodromes, in one case even the signal of a radio direction-finding beacon, were apparently being transformed in the ether, leaving the transmitters in their intended form but reaching Garland's monitoring receivers, sometimes only a couple of hundred miles away, as a single homogenised note.

After two days of continuous monotone, the sound began to be broken up in such a way as to produce dots and dashes: Morse code in fact. But all the Morse said was:

.--/.-/.. /.-../...

which spells out:

W-A-I-L-S.

Naturally they investigated the possibility that it was an elaborately pointless practical joke. But it was certain that radio transmissions were being converted into Morse signals in the atmosphere, without the use of any kind of electronic device. The scientific knowledge required to do this, and the extent of the phenomenon, which was occurring simultaneously all over the northern hemisphere, was far beyond the means of any private individual.

Meetings were arranged in great secrecy and at the highest level: one in Washington, another in Tokyo. In spite of the many alternative hypotheses, most of the time at these meetings was spent discussing the theory put forward by Chief of Staff of the Bundeswehr, that an important message from the whales was imminent. The spelling W-A-I-L-S caused some confusion (the Prime Minister of France pointed out that in French the word for whale was *baleine*) but there was no real opposition to the view that, for the first time in recorded history, a non-human species was attempting to communicate in human terms.

A week ago the conversion of randomly chosen transmissions into the Morse signal W-A-I-L-S had ceased. There were unprecedentedly heavy blizzards all along the eastern seaboard of the United States, and in several cities, including Philadelphia, the cutting-off of electricity supplies caused thousands of people to freeze to death. That was also the week of the Stockholm earthquake.

Then a new series of Morse letters began to be picked up: A-M-B-A-S-A-D-O-R-S.

At a secret conference in Paris four days ago, attended by both the President of the United States and the Prime Minister of the Russian Federation, it was decided that any attempt by the whales to arrange some sort of meeting would receive full co-operation.

Then yesterday, simultaneously in nine different countries, monitoring devices picked up the longest Morse message yet. It said: Motor launch. Porthleven. Course South-west. February 20.

'And it gave *your* names, *your* address,' Garland told them. 'I don't suppose you know anything more than we do, but there's a motor launch all ready waiting at Porthleven. That's in Cornwall. South-west takes you straight out into the Atlantic. It's no good arguing or making excuses: the whales have appointed you plenipotentiaries of the human race.'

Below the helicopter the long-forgotten chiaroscuro of green fields and black factories was bleached to a solemnly glittering desert by the months of snow. Twin parallel lines of trees marking the sides of half-buried roads criss-crossed the white blankness like stitching.

There were huge menacing pagodas of cloud piled up on either side but the helicopter seemed to fly spot-lit in a beam of sun which thrust its way through the vapours darkening the west.

'You may think this ridiculous,' said the brigadier. 'Or on the other hand you may already be operating with the whales and know all about it. But at any rate I think the whales know you're on this helicopter flying to Porthleven. And we don't think you'll be in any danger once at sea in the launch. If the whales had any reason for wishing to harm you individually, we believe they could have done so before now.'

'It's true,' said Imogen. 'The whales have chosen us.'

'But why?'

'We don't know,' said the brigadier. 'But it's your names they sent us, so it's you who are going. Look at that.'

They looked out through the plexiglass. It had begun to rain and there were two separate rainbows, two complete arches of luminous colour, one on either side of a lane in which the helicopter flew.

XVIII

Whales, so-called, belong to two great families. They had probably already emerged as two distinct families of primitive land mammals millennia before they had sought superior strength by returning to the waters from which all life had originally sprung. Though similarly adapted to their aquatic environment, the two great families of whale are no more nearly related than a policeman and a police-dog, having already evolved as quite separate species in the middle Miocene period, over twenty million years ago.

Twenty million years is seven times the period that has elapsed since man began to be something different from an ape.

One family of whales, the *Mystacoceti* or whalebone whales, which include the giant blue whale, and the Greenland Right Whales, have no teeth. They catch krill by filtering vast mouthfuls of sea through the sieve-like whalebone formations in their huge mouths. They have symmetrical skulls, with two blow-holes at the top of the head, through which they eject two perpendicular jets of spray which in most species tend to fall to either side, and only the first pair of ribs join the sternum. The females are slightly larger than the males.

The other family, the *Odontoceti* or tooth whales, which include the dolphin, killer whale and sperm whale, have asymmetrical skulls and a single blow-hole, through which they blow with a forward slant, though generally one sees a mist rather than a distinct spout. Several pairs of ribs join the sternum. The male is much bigger than the female.

The tooth whales, as beasts of prey – in some cases preying on whalebone whales – are much the more scheming and enterprising.

But it was the whalebone whales, which for millions of years had grazed on the moving banks of krill, fol-lowing the migrations of these underwater multitudes as they drifted with the seasons and the currents, who had learnt to understand the weather, and the factors which controlled it. It was they, judiciously moving floods of krill so as to adjust and alter the temperature of the ocean, who had learnt how to seed clouds. It was they who caused the phenomenon known as El Niño, where unusually warm water off the coast of Peru causes a decline of pressure over the eastern Pacific, with a rise of pressure over Australia and the reversal of wind directions along the equator, thus affecting weather conditions even on the eastern seaboard of the United States.

And once they knew how to seed clouds and reverse wind direction, it was only a question of time before they learnt how to raise tempests and sow whirlwinds.

XIX

The sun, now an incandescent orange ball, began to bite into the horizon, and a crimson trackway spilt out from it and crossed the gently rippling waters to their launch. Behind them the harbour buildings were uniformly topped with tea-cosies of snow and barricaded by the stalactites of ice hanging from their gutters; ahead the silver-grey sea was as uncluttered as a Swedish serving dish.

Their departure was like a cross between Salvador Dali and Claude Lorrain: the departure of the Queen of Sheba into the dawn in a Vosper motor boat.

A second launch, with a crew of over-armed policemen, escorted them to a point five miles out to sea.

*

Hove to, the launch wallowed between the waves in a disagreeable manner, so that he was obliged to open up the throttle merely to settle his stomach. It was rapidly growing darker. Behind them he could see the green navigation lamp of the other launch as it sped back to the shore, and, beyond, various pinpoints of light on the land. Ahead, apart from some odd patches of luminescence on the water, there was only the afterglow.

Their whole day had been so amazing that he had no clear idea of anything, except that he had no intention of obeying the brigadier's instructions.

'They're right, you know,' Imogen said. 'We are equally in the whales' power wherever we are, so we are no worse off here than anywhere else.'

'At least the ants can't get us,' he said, aware of an unevenness in his voice that made him wonder whether this remark sounded like light-heartedness or hysteria.

Imogen had never been out to sea before. She looked around with pleasure. 'It's like mathematics,' she said, 'the way the wrinkling of the sides of the waves into miniature crests and valleys perfectly reproduces the crests and valleys of the waves themselves.' She did not seem upset by the thought that the immensity of salt water on either side and – even worse – underneath harboured legions of calculating whales.

In any case, she said that all she could detect was the mental and metabolic activity of a pair of dolphins following thirty yards behind.

As far as he was concerned, though, on a scale for measuring dire situations from one to ten, this one scored sixty-seven and a half. But to avoid argument he waited until Imogen had gone inside the cabin before spinning the wheel to change course.

It had no effect. They continued undeviatingly south-west.

Imogen reappeared, with a yellow sou'wester on her head.

'Some food if you want it, and lots of clothes.'

'We might as well turn in,' he said numbly, thinking: the steering might be repairable, but not in the dark. He said, 'Or I suppose we have to keep watch in turns in case we run into something.'

'I'll see to that,' said Imogen. 'You sleep.'

She seemed excessively cheerful.

'You know, I was getting very bored at the zoo,' she confided ingenuously. 'I was settling down too much to a domestic routine with you – had stopped thinking in terms of what I wanted – not that I knew – it always had to be what *we* wanted. And I want to be free.'

'Free to do what?' he asked, running out of patience.

'Freedom is the freedom not simply to do but to be

oneself. Perhaps I could be anything I wanted – only I have to know what I want. I don't think I was finding that out, living with you.'

He tried to concentrate on what she was saying. All he could see of her face was her eager low-nosed profile under the sou'wester.

'Perhaps I should have left you if nothing had happened. Now it's a bit more like when we were escaping from the Institute. I find I like being with you more when it's like this.'

'Like when I'm being terrified out of my wits?'

But her words distracted him a little.

'Would you really have left me? Were you that fed up with me?'

'Not fed up with you. It was just that you were making things too easy for me. It was too easy just being your woman.'

'*Were* you my woman?'

'Now I don't know what is going to happen and the only familiar thing around is *you*. All things change and behind them is a purpose.'

'Was it *you* who interfered with the steering?'

'Me?'

She looked surprised, swung round with a jerk and, grabbing the wheel, spun it in both directions.

'This must be *their* doing. The whales. Not mine.'

'I may be able to repair it in the morning.'

'I don't think we should worry too much. We go where the whales want us to go. Don't you think it will be interesting?'

'You're so full of shit your eyes are brown. All I want is to get back to land.'

'Well, I think it's interesting. I like it. You go to sleep. I promise to wake you if I see a whale.'

She blew him a kiss, an annoying gesture in the circumstances, though he wondered where she had picked it up.

In the darkness the sea was an invisible presence. The stars were beginning to come out, each one an eye watching them across the light years. There is a star in the Milky Way for every man that ever lived. The launch reverberated gently as it sped south-west.

*

When he woke it was to hear a rattling of pots in the little galley immediately beyond the head of his berth. The launch seemed to be pitching more than the previous evening. Imogen, wearing a long seaman's jersey and seemingly nothing else, came from the galley with a mug of coffee.

'Nothing to report,' she said. 'Scrambled eggs or fried?'

Imogen with long legs, calf muscles outlined in millimetric black fuzz.

'Fried.'

He went aft to the cockpit. There was a brisk wind which whipped ribbons of foam from the crests of the waves, but it was from dead astern and merely increased their speed through water. The horizon, dilating and contracting like the pulsations of a primitive heart, seemed very close – he had never before been out to sea in such a small vessel.

'Are the dolphins still following?' he asked.

'They were relieved during the night. There's two of something else, from their energy presence they seem to be bigger and more intelligent but they haven't shown themselves so I'm not sure what they are.'

He scanned the horizon. The moon, not yet set, was a white smudged postmark to the west. To the north clouds were building up. There was something about one particular cloud: he kept looking at it. There was nothing special about the shape: it was just that it somehow seemed to be in charge of the other clouds.

Then he saw something rather strange: for a few moments the dead body of a policeman floated alongside. It even bumped against the hull. Judging by his helmet and goggles it was one of the policemen from the other launch. As the corpse fell astern the propeller wash caused it to change position in the water, and the last he saw of it was a hand reaching up out of the water, as if trying to halt the spindrift.

After he had eaten breakfast he examined the steering. The tiller was housed in a casing in the stern with an inspection hatch fastened with screws. He found a toolbox, with a screwdriver and spanners, and unscrewed the hatch. The steering cables were not fastened to the rudder head: they seemed to have been cut off with an acetylene torch. There was a quantity of wire in the toolbox and with this he reconnected the steering. He was just screwing the inspection cover back – he anticipated that the launch would pitch more and perhaps ship water once he changed course, so he decided to replace the hatch first – he was just tightening the last screw when the engine died.

'Was that you?' he asked angrily.

'No. Perhaps it was the whales. Look.'

She pointed astern. He turned, fearfully expecting to see a whale, but what he actually saw was no less unwelcome: a slick of oil that created a valley of calm astern between the hillocks of choppy waves. Evidently there was a leak in the fuel tank. Quickly he checked. The tank was half-full: of oily sea-water.

Despite the choppiness of the waves, the pitching of the launch had not increased, and he had the impression the launch was actually moving forward.

At first he discounted the twelve knots shown on the speedometer, but they soon left their oil slick behind and sometimes, though the wind seemed to be from astern, he felt a slipstream in his face when he looked forward. Since there were no fixed objects in sight it was difficult to prove they were moving, till finally a seagull appeared astern, and after keeping stationary for ten minutes began to drop behind, even though flying in the same direction as the launch was pointing.

'The whales are in charge,' said Imogen contentedly, propping her elbows on the roof of the cabin and gazing forward.

*

Meanwhile, clouds had been piling up to the north: dark luminous clouds, unnatural purposeful-looking clouds that were creeping inexorably closer.

The sea was becoming much choppier. The horizon altered its slant every moment. Occasional spurts of salt-flavoured wind whipped up swirls of spray from the tops of the waves and flung them across his face.

The sun went out. The clouds were right overhead. It was as gloomy as the onset of night. Rain drops clog-danced on the roof.

The waves were now higher than the boat, but

still gentle, so that though at one moment they were plunged into the depths of a broad valley, with marbled brown hillsides towering to left and right, and the next moment raised up, confronted by an ocean of regular symmetrical mountain peaks as far as the horizon, they seemed to be in no danger; yet the motion was very unpleasant.

'I think we'd better get below and close everything,' he said.

The motion was even more noticeable inside the cabin. Even more unpleasant. And there seemed to be draughts everywhere, blowing through unsuspected cracks. He lay on a bunk, trying to ignore the lurching. The smallness of the cabin was like a coffin.

Suddenly the launch seemed to strike something. It trembled from stem to stern: a frying pan crashed to the galley floor. Imogen's shoes, which she had taken off, foxtrotted from one end of the cabin to the other. The port holes were covered with beads of water: then for a moment the water splashes had gone but the world outside was grey-green.

The floor rose up very fast, like a lift. For a long moment – long enough to count to five – the whole cabin was motionless, as if caught in mid-air. On the count of five it tilted over on its side and dropped.

More loose saucepans hurled themselves at one another in the galley.

Up again. This time they seemed upside-down.

There was a massive blow against the roof. Then up again. They could hear the wind, indignant, forcing itself to howl. The floor tilted again. Another blow. He staggered to the cabin door. He didn't want to be trapped inside when the launch went down. He opened the door to the cockpit.

The sky was as dark as midnight, but a greenish radiance which had descended on all the metal fittings showed the rain slanting down in bitter diagonals. A tattered flash of lightning threw the horizon close against the launch, silhouetting gigantic foam-streaked waves like cliff-sides that were running about in all directions at the speed of express trains, occasionally colliding and hurling themselves together high in the air, though the wind drowned out all other sounds so that this frenzy of movement took place to a soundtrack that was stuck and tearing. The largest wave of all seemed to be racing straight towards them. He slammed the door just in time to feel it shake in his grasp as if a huge fist had struck it. Then they were going down, nose first, so suddenly that he was thrown across the cabin. He tasted blood in his mouth.

Imogen was in one of the bunks, watching him. Her face glowed.

XX

Whales of course don't mind storms. They are more seaworthy than even the most up-to-date police launch, and they are in very little danger of drowning. When they blow, the out-rush of used-up air is under so much pressure that it will blast through even a wave breaking squarely over the beast's head.

Breathing in is a little more tricky. Whales can inhale hundreds of litres of air in a few one-second snorts and in an average-force gale they tend merely to wallow in the troughs between the waves, timing their inhalations to coincide with the moments when water is not breaking over their heads, but in really violent weather, when everything is monstrously speeded-up and there is a real danger of snorting down a hundred-weight of salt water, one of the most wonderful sights in nature is to see them surfing on the crests of

200-foot waves, occasionally leaping into the air like partridges when two waves collide.

The round-the-world yachtsman Arthur Gibb-Stradling recounts that during a storm off Cape Horn, as his fifty-foot ketch rose on one of the most tremendous waves he had ever encountered, he saw through the stinging spray two whales keeping station on either side of his boat, at a distance of about twenty yards. One of them, he says, rolled 45° on its axis revealing 'a little piggy eye that seemed to observe one's predicament with derision, and a mouth large enough to swallow a main-mast sideways'. As they coasted abreast down the side of the wave Gibb-Stradling saw that the whales were not moving parallel to the forward sweep of the wave but were running directly before the wind, just as he was trying to do, though while in his case it was obviously a losing struggle, for them it seemed to require no visible effort. He seemed to be moving ahead faster, if much less buoyantly, than the two huge creatures, but a second before their wave crashed into another roller their tails flipped up out of the water and the next thing he knew they were shooting through the air past him, like dolphins, though with a flatter trajectory in their leap. As his water-laden boat staggered level with them again the whale on his left sounded but the one on the right continued alongside for another minute and a half. Then, before it disappeared into the depths, it nudged the side of his prow with its huge nose, which Gibb-Stradling describes as 'very much like the largest india-rubber in the world', bringing his stern more directly into the wind, something he had been unable to achieve by means of his helm. 'It had clearly perceived how important it was for one not to come beam-on to the wind, and how difficult it was, with the wind gusting at up to 150 m.p.h., to hold a safe course,' the yachtsman told reporters after his return to Plymouth. 'But what particularly impressed one was that they seemed as much at home in that frightful weather as a swift in a stiffish breeze.'

XXI

About a week after the tempest it became warm
enough for Imogen to sunbathe on the roof of the
cabin. There was only room for one person to lie
diagonally, and he would stand in the cockpit, leaning
against the edge of the roof beside her head with his
cheek tickled by her Afro, looking at her flattened
Pepsi-Cola-coloured breasts and crop of corkscrewy
pubic hair and her legs tapering in perspective away
from him.

At night she would sit on the cabin roof hugging
her knees and obediently turning her face this way and
that as he pointed to Orion, Sirius, Polaris, Regulus,
Andromeda, Cassiopeia, Aldebaran, the Pleiades, Cor
Caroli, Ras Algethi. They could see all the constel-
lations he had learnt as a teenager, plus extra ones,
like the last wreaths of dispersing mist, crowding in

the infinite depths between and beyond the brighter stars. It was like looking not up but down from a great height at the lights of thousand upon thousand of villages scattered across the peaks and ridges and down in the valleys and canyons of a frontierless continent.

'You can feel each million miles as if you had to walk it,' she said. 'Tsin Hsuan writes somewhere that eternity is the time it takes to walk from one side of the universe to the other.'

'Who's Tsin Hsuan?'

'Of course the universe is expanding faster than you or I could walk.'

Around them the sea was a constant presence, moving indiscernibly though with occasional patches of phosphorescence like the reflection of the galaxies overhead: sometimes there would be answering patches of whitish-green light in the northern sky, hanging vertically and trembling like ribbons shaken by a vast wind; he guessed this must be the *aurora borealis*, though they were far below the latitudes where it was normally visible.

Once he saw a moving light which he thought was an aeroplane, but it turned out to be a meteor. Sometimes there were whole showers of meteors, but never once did they see a plane.

The compass showed they were still heading southwest. On each successive night there seemed to be

115

more stars in the sky than on the previous night, and each day was brighter and calmer and hotter than the day before.

One evening Imogen turned in earlier than usual and in the morning she remained in her bunk when he got up, though he could see the whites of her eyes in the gloom of the cabin.

'I'm sorry,' she said. 'I thought, being black, it wouldn't matter being in the sun so much. But it's made me ill.'

'Are you sure? You would have felt it yesterday if you had heat-stroke.'

'Not heat-stroke, as such. Organ rejection.' He could feel rather than see the way she was staring up at him, and the effort she was having to make to keep her voice at a natural pitch. 'I can't tell yet, but I think my brain's being rejected by . . . your friend's body.'

Two days before she had asked, 'When are you going to stop looking at my body as if it was something to eat?' Now it was not *my body* but *your friend's body*. *Your friend's* body is rejecting *my* brain.

'Are you sure?'

'Not yet.'

'I mean, how would you be able to tell?'

'The usual symptoms – I'm not even sure I've got any of them yet – are memory lapse, general loss of intellectual power, loss of specific functions like ability to multiply numbers or to explain spatial relationships. At that point a form of blood-poisoning sets in, with blotching of the skin and fever . . . Life can be prolonged by blood drainage and replacement but one doesn't normally survive the third transfusion. It used to happen now and again at the Calloway Institute. They tried to hide what was going on from us but of course it wasn't difficult to get the technicians to speak whenever they were alone with one of us . . . In my case, without transfusion, I shall die within three days. Four days at the most.' She seemed almost proud at being able to explain it so clearly. 'There is often one very beautiful and profound idea or insight before one dies, about twenty-four hours before the end, just before the intellectual functions disintegrate altogether. That was one of the things we used to talk about in the Institute.' By now her voice was little more than a whisper. 'Make sure you write my last idea down. It will be my final good-bye gift to you, a present in return for all you've done for me. I shall be very thirsty but there is not enough water on the boat for what I would drink, not if you are to reach the other side of the sea, so you must promise not to give me *any*.'

By the afternoon she was in a coma. He stayed by her all through the night, and all through the next day, wiping away the sweat which bathed her from every pore, leaving her only to hang out the towels he was using so they could dry in the warm night breeze or, later on, in the sun. When her mattress was drenched, he moved her to the other bunk: the first time he had held her naked body since the night before his arrest. He found himself remembering the other Imogen's razored and talcum-powdered armpits: this Imogen's were luxuriantly unshaved, like sea urchins. He covered her quickly and, exhausted, stretched out on the bare boards of the bunk he had taken her from.

'Goodnight,' she whispered: the first words she had spoken for nearly forty-eight hours. 'Don't try to wake me in the morning.'

He knew then that she was telling him she would die in the night, without even giving him his promised good-bye present of a profound and beautiful thought, and that he was not to take too much notice. He lay listening to the breathing, twice before saved from stopping, that would this time cease for ever during the night, and his eyes smarted, and he slept.

He dreamt that he was hiding from the police and that a girl who refused to show him her face was keeping him alive by bringing him helpings of Christmas pudding, every night when it struck twelve. He knew it was a girl, though she never spoke, because once when reaching out for the Christmas pudding in the dark his groping fingers found a tipped-up resilient little breast and skinny teenage ribs. He kept hoping she would show him her face but she never did, and something prevented him from pulling aside the veil or scarf or whatever it was that hid her features. And since he wanted more than anything to know whether she was someone he already knew, or someone whom he had never encountered before but who would be important in the next phase of his life, he would touch her breast each time she came, expecting that sooner or later she would say in Imogen's voice – the first Imogen's voice – 'Stop mauling me, man,' or, 'Leave my teenies alone.' But she never spoke, though after the first time her nipple was hard as if aroused and ready for his furtive caress, and each time that she came and handed him his Christmas pudding and left without speaking, he became that little bit less sure that he would recognise Imogen's voice if he heard it again, so that he would spend the long hours between the girl's visits trying to remember Imogen's voice, trying to remember particular incidents and what she had said, and how she had said it. He remembered the fire at Dalston Cross for example, and the way the flames had reflected on her face as she looked up at him from the ground, but although he could recall the way her lips had moved, and knew perfectly well that she had spoken, the only sounds that he could recollect were the shouts of the firemen, and a kind of rumbling from the fire, and the grinding of the rubble as it shifted and subsided each time he pulled a bit of it away. The only conversation that he found he could remember properly seemed to have been a few days later; he supposed it must have been during their first evening together at his flat, after he had been thrown out by her mother and Imogen had come with him, to look after him while his hands were still bandaged. He had been already lying in bed, on his back, feverish and light-headed, his hands aching and itching in their gauze wrappings, and Imogen had come in, wearing his best pale-blue shirt as a nightie, and had leaned against the door and said:

'Um, you know, I decided I'd better be sensible and mature and organised about you know, sleeping with you and that, so I checked in your bathroom cabinet if you had any condoms and I found *this*.'

And she had held up one of those extravagantly knobbly spikey mauve condoms one gets through mail order, or from machines in the toilets of the kind of club where you're afraid to go to the toilet: he had found it one day in the gutter and had taken it home because the seal of the packet was still unbroken.

'They're much better for blowing up like balloons than the ordinary sort are,' he had said.

'Dickhead,' she had said. 'Shall we blow it up now

or save it up till, you know, we've tried a packet of the ordinary kind?'

But the more he rehearsed the sound of her voice saying this, the less he was able to recall what she actually looked like, so that he began to be afraid that if the veiled girl spoke at last, and if he recognised her voice and said, 'Imogen!', and she lowered the covering from her face, he would still not know if it was her.

When he woke in the eerie dawn light the only sound to be heard was the lapping and creaking of the sea against the hull, and the stillness and silence in the cabin made him sure Imogen's dead body was lying stiff and cold in the bunk on the other side of the narrow aisle. He lay thinking how much he had hoped from what he had thought was his second chance with the *other* Imogen, and how differently it had turned out: and now she was dead, beyond any possibility of a third life, and it was probably his turn next, since he was after all adrift in a small boat and there was no reason why he should be permitted to live now that she was no longer with him.

'It's all right to give me some water now,' she said suddenly.

'I thought you were dead.'

'No, simply dying for a cup of water.'

'But you said – '

121

'I know: but I was only going on what happened to the others, in the Institute.'

When he returned with the water, she said huskily:

'I guess they didn't want to live as much as I did.'

And she gave him such a radiant smile that tears sprang to his eyes and began trickling embarrassingly down his cheeks.

She watched him intently over the rim of her cup, and as soon as she had emptied it let it slide down to her midriff and began wiping away his tears with her hand. He flinched away from her but was brought up sharp by the bunk behind him. She leant out of her bunk towards him. He closed his eyes.

'On top of all this, it's my period,' he heard her say. 'I think this coming month I'm going to drop a couple of really *big* ova.'

XXII

Meanwhile the launch had continued on its course south west. They were heading for a part of the world which had been populated by humans for less than sixty (perhaps less than twenty) thousand of the world's 4,600 million years, which had never had an Old Stone Age, and which had everywhere been colonised, and in most places repopulated, by more recent migrants from areas where man had lived 200,000 years ago: what we now call Spain, Brittany, Britain but which 200,000 years ago was a kind of hunting frontier reporting back to the vast territories further east which had first given rise to Man.

Humanity's history and prehistory of movement and replacement of populations parallels the unwritable history of the rise, dominance, movement and decline of non-human species, such as the wolf, the starling, the rabbit, HIV.

History, the record of specific events that relate to other specific events, can hardly be said to have existed before the invention of writing, and though scarcely a day passes without the unearthing of human relics older than the oldest literate civilisations, the further back one goes in time the smaller the proportion that survives of early man's detritus and discardings. Marvellous paintings have been found in limestone caves in southern France, but only a tiny minority of early mankind ever made use of caves, because in most of the area inhabited by early man there were no caves to be made use of. The woodland clearings and river banks where early man usually camped have either been buried by sedimentation or eroded away by millennia of winds: it is a rare miracle that brings together a ground surface trodden a thousand centuries ago and a ground surface conveniently accessible to modern archaeologists. For more than a hundred years we have been toying with a jigsaw we have presumptuously labelled *Early Man* but so far we have only found a tiny percentage of the pieces scattered among the compost of the planet's past.

Yet early man too lived in a world of specific events that related to other specific events. Just as history has repeated itself in modern times, so it repeated itself then, and probably much more frequently in the course of a vastly greater time-span. Languages evolved, developed, gave rise to other languages, and became extinct. The languages of modern civilisation have been becoming progressively simpler in their grammar during the last two thousand years: our remote ancestors, like today's (or at least yesterday's) Eskimos and Australian Aboriginals and American Indians spoke languages immensely more complicated in their grammatical structure and morphology than modern English or modern Chinese, yet these languages, like the elaborate Indo-European tongue from which modern English derives, were the result of scores of thousands of years of linguistic evolution from the much simpler grammars and vocabularies employed by pre-Man. Today there are at least half-a-dozen European languages on the verge of extinction, and at least as many that have died out altogether during the past five centuries, but we have no way of knowing how many human languages flourished and then became extinct prior to the invention of writing.

Technologies too have emerged, disseminated themselves and perhaps finally evaporated. Similar needs inspire similar remedies. Just as, in more recent times, the invention of property led everywhere to the invention of police, so in the remote past the existence of narrow streams must have led people thousands of miles and hundreds of centuries apart to hit independently on the idea of using logs as foot-bridges. No doubt many discoveries were made, forgotten, made again, forgotten again, repeatedly during the course of millennia. The secret of how to spread, exploit and even conserve fires caused by lightning was probably learnt and then lost thousands of times. It is even possible that the catapult was separately invented, and separately developed, over successive generations, into the bow and arrow among a number of different tribal groups that had no contact with one another. It is difficult to believe, though, in the simultaneous development, in different parts of the globe, of a weapon so cumbersome as the blow-pipe, which is only effective after long practice and requires a sophisticated knowledge of vegetable poisons: yet two hundred years ago it was found to be in use by the primitive people of both Borneo and Amazonia. And though we can easily believe that our remote ancestors knew how to make use of fires caused by lightning or scorching drought, it is extraordinary enough that even one lot of men should have been able to figure out for themselves that they could *cause* a fire by rubbing pieces of wood together, if only they could invent a technique for rubbing it fast enough: and not at all easy to believe that the same idea should have occurred independently to a number of different groups who knew nothing of one another.

The invention of the blow-pipe and of *man-made* fire were almost certainly as much specific events – and quite as epoch-making – as the invention of gunpowder and steam engines but we have not the least idea where or when or how they happened. Much the greater part – and in some senses also the most mind-boggling part – of human history is as lost to us as the chronology of the mutation, multiplication and migration of animal populations prior to the last few hundred years.

The main reason why we understand so little of what is happening to our world is that we know so little of what has happened in the past.

XXIII

When they awoke on the twenty-ninth day, Imogen saw a shadow of land on the western horizon.

They steered towards the low slate-grey mass. The breeze tugged encouragingly at the makeshift sail they had rigged up. After an hour the greyness began to change colour to liver-green and the contours of two hills became visible; later, a range of jagged mountain peaks crept up far beyond, a wisp of morning fog floating horizontally dividing them from the hills at the coast and making them seem as improbably steep and high as the mountains of the moon.

By the time the sun was vertically overhead in a turquoise sky they were able to see a long white line of surf, and the trunks of trees closely ranked beyond like a palisade almost at the water's edge. And they could hear the surf, a sound like the rumble of an endless goods train passing in the night.

'I'm afraid we might be smashed up on those breakers,' he said. 'We must look for a bay.'

But just as they began to tack, the wind veered and collapsed their little sail. He swung the useless wheel back and forth. Already the beach seemed much closer. The breakers, which had looked a uniform incandescent white, had become broken up into distinct swirls of green and silver. Occasionally, yards above the crests of the waves, rainbows hovered in the spume. Beyond, the trees watched in crowded ranks, as unresponding as policemen.

'Can you swim?'

'I had some lessons,' said Imogen. But her voice was suddenly loud, unnecessarily clear, for a dead silence had exploded around them. The breakers had changed direction: no longer cascading on the beach, the waves had parted and were fleeing from the boat on either side, still creaming and breaking white as snow ten yards away to left and right but leaving a calm path straight ahead. It was as if they were directly behind an enormous invisible ship whose bow wave sent the waters rushing in opposite directions, it was as if wolves were running to left and right leaving open greensward ahead. Behind them the waves came back together in a mighty surge.

The breeze, which had been fresh and pleasant, had suddenly ceased, and where the waves parted there was a dead and wooden calm.

The launch coasted the last few yards and grated on the beach. He jumped out. He had never had such a strong sense of hidden watchers.

'Shouldn't we pull the boat up out of the water?' asked Imogen.

'No.'

Perhaps the path cut through the surf had been more modest than it had seemed from its midst, but there was something particularly redolent of meaning and intention in the way the breakers had returned to their remorselessly leisured crunching, as if to convey that they had been grinding away with unaltered tempo on that beach since the beginning of eternity.

The beach, which curved gradually out of sight to either side, seemed as exposed as the plate on a Beales-Thomas microscope. The only cover was the trees, as close together as the bristles of a brush.

He wanted to dive between the trunks of the two nearest trees and put as much distance between himself and the haunted waters as possible.

'There were some hills,' he said. 'If we could climb to higher ground we could perhaps figure out where we are.'

'There was a hill a bit to the left. We won't be able

to see it among the trees, we had better walk a little way along the beach.'

It was beginning to be very hot and there was a sickly smell of rotting vegetation. The light was almost orange by contrast with the frozen white light of London. Occasional raucous bird calls sounded from the far depths of the forest and there was still that strong unremitting sense of being watched; but nothing moved, only the white zig-zag of foam crawling ceaselessly forwards and backwards all along the beach. They set out in the direction Imogen had suggested.

XXIV

They came to a tract of forest where the trees alongside the beach – palms and custard apple trees and red birch – were about five yards apart. They decided to head inland.

And as they were walking towards the trees he saw a footprint in the sand: saw and passed on without saying anything, alert not to frighten Imogen prematurely. It was not human: a large square print with toes out at the sides.

Soon they were going uphill, stepping in and out of bars and slats of glaring sunlight, with the trees soaring all around like the masts of ships. The forest was completely hushed save for the sighing of the breeze in counterpoint to the dwindling echo of the surf behind them, and the hoots and screechings of birds far ahead and at a great distance on either side.

The stillness near at hand made it seem that some intruding alien presence had temporarily driven out the usual inhabitants of this reach of the wood, though whether that intruder was themselves or something more powerful and more dread that was watching over them, he scarcely dared to wonder.

Finally they came out on a ridge. The sky was as bright as a neon sign. They were not high enough to have any view behind them of the sea: it was still faintly audible but cordoned off from them by the forest they had walked through. In front the land fell away in a kind of shallow amphitheatre. There were one or two trees scattered across the sloping banks where one might have expected to see the cheaper seats, and thickets of shoulder-high shrubbery, some of it bright with yellow flowers; the floor of the amphitheatre looked from where they stood like a tussocky lawn. Beyond it the land rose in a densely wooded hill. The crests of the trees, even on the middle slopes of the hill, were swept back, like icing smoothed by a confectioner's trowel.

'All those plants!' Imogen exclaimed. Until that morning she had never seen flowering plants growing in the open air.

He plucked a blade of coarse grass and showed her how to blow through it so as to make a noise halfway between a fart and a whistle. She laughed, and he had a sudden uncomfortable recollection of once showing someone else the same trick.

'Let's get on,' he said.

The descent of the shallowly sloping bank was not difficult; they even found what appeared to be an animal track, which skirted the densest thickets. Halfway down they began to see enormous blue dragon-flies and clouds of mosquitoes dancing in regiments just above their heads, though somehow they were not bitten once. But the floor of the amphitheatre turned out to be a morass, strewn with half-decayed tree trunks.

'Crocodiles?' he suggested.

'I'm afraid so,' said Imogen. 'I recognise their brain patterns from the zoo.'

They tried to find a route around the edge of the swamp. After breasting through the flowering shrubs for a couple of minutes they came to a huge tree which had been blown over on its side right across the marshy area, providing a causeway three feet above the level of the mire. They crossed on this and began to ascend the opposite slope. The bird cries still seemed very distant, drowned out by the sound of insects incessantly stopping and starting, like tiny machines, in the surrounding foliage. The huge dragon-flies approached, hovered, and darted away: it seemed as if they never saw the same one twice.

It was now unpleasantly hot, and damp, and sticky.

The trees provided shelter from the direct blast of the sun but also held off the sea breeze, and they walked through a hot inert sweaty darkness that seemed to resist their movements as much as water.

At last they came to the top of the hill. There was no clear view of the sea because of the sloped-back tops of the trees rooted lower down the hillside, though the infrequent gaps in the dense greenery presented glimpses of shimmering aquamarine, or an occasional view of an empty horizon. But on the landward side they soon came to a spot where the collapse of part of the hillside had created a kind of cliff, with the nearest trees growing far below, and they could look out over a sea of salad, an eternity of vivid undulating green so rich and emphatic in its greenness that it looked as if it had taken all the millions of years of evolution up to that morning to achieve such richness and verdancy and it would never be achieved again. Close to hand the pointillist effect of all those millions of perfect leaves gave the surface of the jungle a 3-D effect; further off it blended into a dense uniform blanket, like green snow. To their left the sun flashed on water, a river or lake; there was much more green blanket beyond. And, on the far side of this universe of trees, showing amethyst in the hallucinatory brightness of the noon sun, hovered a range of mountains, ramparts from left to right across the opposite horizon.

XXV

It should not have surprised anyone that the whales could not spell correctly.

It was astonishing that creatures without hands or manipulation could grasp the principle of forming letters and writing. The biggest mystery is how they had access to a sufficient quantity of printed material for purposes of analysis.

They had obviously managed to penetrate the workings of the world political system, hence their choosing to communicate in English.

The intermediate stages whereby whale intelligence attained a penetration of human culture almost certainly implies a mastery of the intervening animal stages.

A degree of communication between different species of warm-blooded creatures is not unknown. Various types of hornbill keep company with zebras, bustards, even arboreal monkeys, in order to prey on the insects dislodged by the large animals as they feed, and it seems the larger creatures tolerate the smaller because the sharp eyes of the hornbill provide extra security against predators. The oxpecker or tickbird, which perches on the back of African rhinoceroses or on the necks of giraffes, searching for ticks, sometimes warns its host of possible danger by hissing but at other times shows signs of alarm only when its host turns its neck to observe the approach of an intruder. In Europe birds like the reed bunting, blackbird, blue tit, great tit and chaffinch all make an almost identical high whistle, very difficult to locate, when a bird of prey flies overhead, and these warnings are evidently recognised by several different species. Smaller seed- or insect-eating birds of different types also make a very similar cry when ganging up against, or 'mobbing', owls or crows. In the confined eco-system of municipal parks one even used to see, now and again, domestic chickens, ornamental ducks and wild geese joining with sparrows and robins to raise the alarm when a cat climbed into the animal enclosure to stalk the young chickens. The magpies and crows would join in too, and the fallow deer would respond to the alarm call of the birds by trotting over in a group to drive the cat away. Not that this implies the communication of very complex information, but much of the information communicated by human speech is routinely obvious, and the faculty of speech may have prevented humans from learning how much could be communicated without it.

XXVI

They decided to head for the mountains.

As they began to scramble down the hillside there was a sudden change in the quality of the air and the outline of objects seemed to become more distinct, as if they were now viewing things through Beales-Thomas lenses. The mosquitoes began to settle and bite, and though Imogen soon found an animal track, brambles and creepers constantly snatched at their shoulders and at the backs of their heads. Before long he had blood running down the side of his face, with never less than a dozen insects swarming in it. A twenty-yard stretch of knee-high grass left them with scores of leeches on their shins and they had to stop to peel them off. Then Imogen announced that they were being followed.

'By what?'

'Lots of things.'

And suddenly, as if at the flick of a switch, the birds which hitherto had been audible only in the far distance began to screech and whistle all around them, deafeningly close but still invisible.

The ground on either side of the track had become marshy, and the trees were scattered on isolated knolls and along the edge of the track itself, which followed a low ridge. The main vegetation nearby consisted of huge reeds and ferns and a low-spreading, evil-smelling shrub with enormous flowers. The racket from the invisible birds was so loud that they heard the crashing among the reeds only at the very last moment, a split second before two crocodiles burst on to the track behind them.

'Run!' he shouted.

The reeds and shrubs seemed to catch at their knees as they sprinted forward. For a moment they could hear the stumbling of the huge creatures behind them, then they were clear.

'There's lots of other things, too,' said Imogen, panting. She did not seem frightened, but her cheek was bleeding from a scratch, and she looked cross.

He snatched up a club-sized stick which lay in their way. For a moment he regretted it: Imogen continued to run, and the stick incommoded him as he tried to keep up with her. He was just about to throw it away when a black creature as big as a man launched itself from a branch high overhead on to Imogen's shoulders, toppling her into the dirt. He smashed his club down on the upper part of the creature's body – it was a black jaguar, *Felis onca*, he recognised it from the zoo – and to his surprise it fell off Imogen and turned to face him with flattened twitching ears and bared fangs. Its eye teeth seemed as long as his fore-finger. Perhaps half-stunned, it was not quick enough to block a second blow with its massive paw, yet it hardly winced as his club smashed into the side of its head. Instead it twisted, still crouching, the end of its tail twitching convulsively, and looked over its shoulder directly into Imogen's eyes. She lay on her side, staring back. As he raised his stick for a third blow at the animal it gathered itself, gave an odd sobbing mew like a frightened cat, and bounded into the cover of the reeds.

Imogen struggled to her feet. She had a deep scratch on one fore-arm, and her blouse was ripped off one shoulder, just like in the cover-picture of a 1950s trash novel.

'Come on,' she said.

They sprinted another hundred yards to a point where the forest on either side became thicker. Fortunately the track was quite wide, so they could keep running. Then they came to a stretch where the denseness of the trees and perhaps a peculiarity of the soil had completely eliminated undergrowth. It was gloomy because of the dense vegetation overhead, though between the tree trunks to either side they could see more tree trunks and yet more tree trunks, almost it seemed to infinity, with occasional sunbeams falling through to the ground like spotlights. Branches and coconuts began to rain down on them; looking up he could see small shadowy figures high overhead, leaping from tree to tree.

Gasping for breath in the hot dank air, they ran on, till they came out on the edge of a broad lake. The expanse of water seemed completely stagnant: here and there were half-submerged branches festooned with slime, and rotting logs sprouting worm-eaten fungi like Modigliani masks. The water glittered where the sun caught it, but it was with an over-rich emerald glow: a miasma of corruption hung over the lake, and suspended in it, vast cathedral-like tiers of mosquitoes which began to close in on the two travellers.

'There's crocodiles too,' said Imogen. 'We should find another route.'

'All these animals, they don't *usually* attack humans, do they?' he asked.

Human civilisation could not protect them any more: this was one of the places where the animals were in charge, hunting human fugitives at will.

Soon the monkeys were bombarding them again as they trudged through the thicket parallel to the margin of the lake. Imogen was attacked by a snake, which lodged its fangs in the leather of her shoe. They were followed for about a mile by a jaguar, which was then joined by another one: with practice Imogen could easily detect and identify large animals by their energy presence. The two jaguars followed them doggedly for about an hour, once or twice slinking into view further down the track. Then they disappeared and the two Ambassadors of the Human Race came to a relatively open space, with only a few trees and flowering bushes.

Rooting among the bushes were lean muscular pigs of a farmyard species long since returned to the wild: some of them had small but sharp tusks. When they saw the two humans they began to close in, and were not discouraged when he threw a stone at the nearest one.

The two of them scrambled up on to a low shelf of rock in order to deal better with the pigs, and their slightly increased elevation enabled them to see the mountains now much closer at hand through a gap in the trees.

He spoke to the animals, saying, 'Greetings, Pigs' – not so easy with a dry mouth.

Some of the boars tried to clamber up on to the shelf of rock but were easily discouraged by kicks to the snout. One more than averagely athletic specimen managed to get a foothold at the furthest end of the ledge but as soon as Imogen turned to deal with it, it lost its footing and fell out of sight with a shrill squealing. It was not hurt but the other pigs desisted from their attack and gathered around the defeated champion. He knew then that it had fallen because Imogen had looked at it, that the jaguar had run away because she had looked at it, that she had the ability to project the force of her mind so as to control everything around her; and he suddenly remembered that the explosion at Dalston Cross had come just as the other Imogen had seen him watching her and scowled.

He began to gather loose rocks with which to bombard their besiegers. After a tense half hour the whole herd suddenly ran away as if at a signal.

He was now completely exhausted and so was Imogen, but they both thought it unlikely they would find any safe shelter till they reached the mountains. Through the trees the folds and pleats of the nearer foothills were alluringly sun-lit: those further away were in shadow as if the light he and Imogen stood in could not reach. After a brief rest they pressed on.

Several of the trees they passed bore fruit but the

only ones he recognised were mangoes and bananas. He picked some and they ate as they walked.

Seeing her with mango juice running over her chin suddenly gave him a very strong reminiscence of the Imogen of five years ago, the other Imogen, and when, taking off one of her trainers to extricate a sharp stone, she put her hand on his shoulder to steady herself, he thought: she's going to kiss me.

She didn't. Instead she said:

'I think these mangoes are giving me the colly-wobbles.'

XXVII

Plants have their history, just like humans and beasts. In fact many of the commonest plants have been established in different parts of the world only by considerable effort on the part of human beings. The banana originated in India, where it was noticed by Alexander the Great in the fourth century BC, but by the time Columbus rediscovered the Americas it was established as far west as the Canary Islands. It was one of the first Old World plants in modern times to make the transfer to the New World. On the other hand the mango, also Indian – according to legend Buddha was given a mango grove so he could rest in its shade – had seeds that did not take kindly to storage and transportation, and it was only after repeated attempts that horticulturalists were able to establish it in Brazil around 1700. From Brazil it spread to the Caribbean during the course of the eighteenth century. Even today it is probable that the majority of mango trees one sees in that area have been deliberately planted: not just those in the gardens of police inspectors, but even those on the slopes of Morne Diablotin and Pico Duarte.

Archaeologists believe man began to cultivate the soil about seven thousand years before Christ, in what is now Iran, Iraq, Syria and south-eastern Turkey, but he had always been a gatherer of plants, having become a hunter of medium-sized animals only at a comparatively late stage of his evolution, perhaps a million or so years ago. It seems likely that he had known which plants produced edible fruit or shoots, at which seasons, from the very earliest period of his development; today gorillas, chimpanzees and even baboons understand the seasonal productivity of plants and have their own strategies for harvesting crops. Early man may well have understood the principles of systematic harvesting, including sorting and storage, tens of millennia before he began to bother with ploughing, sowing and irrigation, and probably began introducing plant species into new habitats long before he realised that such an experiment would work better if sowing or replanting was preceded by ploughing and followed up by weeding and watering.

The bottle gourd, for example, originated in Africa but was being utilised as a container in what is now Mexico by 7000 BC: the seeds, perhaps actually carried in hollowed gourds, may well have crossed the land bridge between Asia and Alaska with the first men to penetrate into the Americas. The first cereal crops cultivated in south-western Asia were einkorn wheat, emmer wheat and wild barley: wild barley occurs naturally all over the area in question and einkorn wheat (*Triticum monococcum*) is a modified form of a wild wheat found from southern Anatolia to the valleys of the Jordan and the lower Euphrates, but emmer wheat (*Triticum dicoccum*) is found in its natural form only in the south-western part of the zone of its early cultivation, so it seems likely that by the date of the earliest archaeological evidence of man's use of emmer wheat he already had long experience of exploiting it more or less systematically.

The principle of burning down tracts of natural vegetation in order to encourage the growth of useful plants was probably understood during the Lower Palaeolithic and was practised millennia ago by communities such as the Australian aboriginals who made little subsequent progress in crop cultivation, but it is possible that humans played a part in how plants were distributed over the globe's surface tens of thousands of years before they had the least notion of actively contributing to the process, even by such crude methods as setting fire to the bush. In fact human consciousness may have had very little to do with some of man's most important contributions to his prehistoric habitat. It occurs often enough in nature that animal species are responsible for spreading plant types. It is only from the human point of view that the relationship of humans and plants is from first to last determined by humans. The Mango evolved much further back in time than Man.

XXVIII

It was already growing dark when, after walking uphill through the forest for some time, they came to the margin of the trees and found ahead of them a landscape of colossal boulders piled up on top of one another and decorated with stunted shrubs. With her ability to detect where other living creatures had been, Imogen soon found a track, which they followed till the moon began to rise. He was now so fatigued that he blundered into obstacles at every step. To add to his discomfort they could hear dogs howling somewhere in the distance. When Imogen noticed a cave they decided to stop for the night.

He had the feeling that someone was in the depths of the cave wanting to speak to them, a sensation so strong that he called out, 'Who is it?' expecting to hear a voice he knew replying. But there was only silence in the interior of the cave, and Imogen shook her head.

'There's only me here . . . At least, there's nothing that can harm us . . . There *is* something, I can even feel that it's somehow friendly but it's definitely not responding to our presence.'

They gathered wood from a strangely scattered copse on the hillside, and lit a fire outside the cave's mouth. The cave, seemingly gouged out of the earth by time, was very small, save for some extensive shelves high up at the back: they had to lie down with their feet almost in the fire. And the copse only provided dry wood: they had to stretch out on the bare, cool rock floor.

Before they fell asleep, Imogen said:

'At least I took your mind off the real Imogen.'

It was as if she had somehow divined that since their departure from England, or at least since her illness in mid-Atlantic, memories of the other Imogen, of that poor sweet kid who had been snatched from him while he had been in jail, had been recurring to him with increasing frequency. As he dozed off he heard the renewed murmuring of her voice, which was not quite the first Imogen's voice and yet did not quite belong to the second Imogen either. She was telling him:

'I am proud to have had you relate to me like a whole woman.'

But, as he dozed off, it was of the other Imogen he was thinking.

*

He woke once or twice from uneasy slumber to see shadows slinking back and forth in the darkness beyond the fire. Not all the wood was quite dry and it burnt slowly, but once he had to get up to throw more branches on the dwindling flames, and he distinctly saw two creatures like great grey dogs pacing among the shadows and the boulders a few yards away.

Re-entering the cave he had to pause to give his eyes time to get used to the dark. As he peered into the surrounding blackness he could sense people both lying and standing beside him. After a minute the flickering light from beyond the entrance picked out a full-lipped mouth on the ground near his feet, and a slant-nostrilled underside of a nose, just as he had seen them picked out by the flames at Dalston Cross.

'This is one of those times I think I like men who are good at taking charge,' the other Imogen had said, flat on her back in the twilight of the burning shopping precinct.

'In that case you won't mind lying back and thinking of England,' he had said.

He put out his hand and groped around near the floor till he encountered the warmth of Imogen's – he wasn't sure which bit of her it was, except that it was too soft to be her shoulder or elbow. As he settled himself again on the hard ground he could hear her talking in her sleep.

It was the first time he had heard her talk in her sleep. She kept repeating: 'It's nice . . . it's nice.'

As he fell asleep he was thinking: it sounds as if she's remembering having sex with someone.

And a moment or two later it seemed to him that he was crouching on top of her, a tit in each hand, and she was humping up at him, legs akimbo, oohing and ah-haha-ing as if someone was trickling ice cubes down her back on the hottest day of the year: he had a fading memory of that other Imogen asking once, 'Am I supposed to make noises like in American movies?'

In the morning they woke simultaneously. Imogen stretched kittenishly.

'Now I'm hungry,' she said.

He stood up. The cave was a different shape from what they had supposed, with an enormously high ceiling, like a funnel, sloping away from the cave's mouth. The sun, moving across the side of the mountains, suddenly flooded the cave mouth with light, enabling him to see the interior better. At the back, standing on a shelf at eye-level, and with their heads lost in shadows and cobwebs ten feet from the floor, were a line of mummified corpses: other travellers long since journeyed across the gulf of time. A couple of them had the bindings of their legs partly unravelled, and the skeletons of two rats lay on the shelf nearby.

They climbed for the best part of the day. Around noon they came to a completely open rock face, so steep they could make progress only with the help of their hands, and halfway up they attracted the attention of four huge vultures which, after circling close enough for them to be able to smell their stench and to hear the click of their pinions as they swerved in the air, began slashing at their backs with enormous hooked talons. Imogen was gashed nastily but once he had found a ledge where he could turn and lash out at the monsters they kept their distance, gliding in circles stiff-winged, like World War II bombers soaring over a column of refugees: somehow reminiscent of police helicopters for all that they were vastly older, as if a primeval prototype. They were still in this exposed area when a tremendous thunderstorm broke out: crashes and booms as if the mountains were breaking up, electric fire sparking among the rocks and running in livid zig-zagging rivulets down the mountain side, even a rock-fall triggered off by lightning striking higher up, with boulders as big as crashing Ferraris bounding and bouncing to right and left. In between the electricity there were deluges of hailstones as large as peas.

Imogen's blouse and bra had been shredded by the vultures, and he gave her his shirt as they crouched under a jutting rock. She half-turned her back as she took off the ruins of her blouse, her shoulder blades moving like the buds of wings. And he could see the figure six-shaped profile of one breast. It had turned bitterly cold so that her skin was all goose-pimples and the teats of her breasts stuck out, two icy black baby's fingers pointing up at 45°, set in goose-pimpled rings. He reached out and touched the nearest, and as she pushed away his hand she caressed it with her hair, flicking her head while fixing him with her earnest round-eyed look.

'Hey, lover boy,' she said. 'That breast doesn't need any more massage. It's my poor old bum that's covered in bruises.'

*

The last few yards to the summit were the steepest and most difficult and they were both in the act of scrambling on to the top of the narrow ridge before they had time to glance at what lay beyond.

The surprise of it unpleasantly reinforced its physically blinding glitter.

155

The sea.

They stood looking out over the open water. There was not even another island in sight. The unflagging salty breeze in their face was like the breath of the whales.

About a mile to their left, and dizzying thousands of feet below, a host of roofs clustered around the margin of a bay which was enclosed between the ridge of mountains they stood on and a secondary ridge running at an angle and terminating in what looked like an extinct volcano. Smoke from cooking fires hung in a grey film over the township.

He felt bitter. There was no going back. The interior of the island was far more immediately hazardous than the open waters. In fact that seemed to be what the whales meant to tell them: that their power extended far inland, and that their victims might just as well stay by the sea.

'I'm starving,' said Imogen. 'We'd better go down.'

XXIX

It did not take long to pick up a track leading down to the village. A few yards below the mountain crest a brownish-grey bird with white markings on its wings and tail was singing energetically on the dead stump of a tree. It did not desist as they approached, and fell silent only when Imogen took it in her hand.

'It's a northern mockingbird,' she said: she had spent a lot of time in the aviaries at the zoo.

'I think it's also called the Jamaican nightingale,' he said, recognising it from the print which had used to be – perhaps still was? – in the Campbells' hall.

'Oh, and here's a path,' Imogen said: at that the bird flew out of her hand, but it kept close to them as they began to make their way down the steep pathway, fluttering from bush to bush in their wake, and occasionally pausing to utter a few bars of song.

In less than two hours they were walking among shacks of rusty corrugated iron patched with Coca-cola tins and polythene and could hear the rumble of surf somewhere ahead.

A few children came out to stare at them. One of the older ones, dressed in tattered underpants and sun-glasses, shouted what sounded like *Raas!* half-heartedly. Fat bespectacled women sat by the dirt track sunning themselves in bright dresses, swatting occasionally at circling flies; sometimes they called *Buenos dias!* Gardeners sitting on kerbstones seemed not to notice them. The people seemed to be off-Miami Americans in broken-down Bermuda shorts and surfing tops. They saw a party of men in dreadlocks marching in almost military order towards the water-front.

Then the drumming started.

At first it was only two or three drums, giving out an even, regular beat like a fast metronome, but loud enough to silence every other noise in the squalid alley-ways. Other drums joined in, perfectly in time. The whole township began to throb and vibrate. From out of the huts people – mainly women and children – began to stream towards the waterfront, pushing past the two travellers with serious preoccupied faces. He tried to ask one scarlet-clad matron where he could buy some food but she brushed past him without even glancing at his face. They came to a hut with sacks of grain stacked outside, and through the door a glimpse of untidy shelves sparingly decorated with tins of food and piles of camouflaged army-surplus bush hats: but if this was a shop, there was no-one there to serve them. The drumming continued at the same even, unbearably loud tempo. Soon the streets were deserted save for one ancient underdressed Chinaman huddled over a carved walking stick, shuffling his bare feet as fast as he could in the direction of the sea.

The two Ambassadors of the Human Race overtook the old man, turned a corner between a derelict bus and a grove of banana palms, and found themselves at the rear of an enormous crowd of people who stood twenty or thirty deep on a slope overlooking the bay. Because of the slope they could see the water over the dreadlocks of the islanders in front, and, right down by the water's edge, the younger men of the township in a double row, banging their drums in unison.

The entire crowd watched the water expectantly. It was quite five minutes before he saw anything at all in the water: then he saw, close to the drummers, in less than six feet of water, a killer whale flit past, its huge black dorsal fin on a level with the drummers' eyes: but they seemed to pay it no attention, and did not alter the rhythm of their drumming.

The bay was about five hundred yards across and

the high ground surrounding it on the landward side made it a natural auditorium: Imogen told him later that the drumming caused an echo from the side of the extinct volcano across the bay, and that the drumming was regulated by the period of the echo, the echo of one beat coinciding perfectly with the beat which followed. Apart from the drumming there was not the slightest noise: those not drumming stared with hypnotised attention at the turquoise waters of the bay.

Then the drumming stopped.

The entire crowd fell to its knees in a single movement, as if standing together on the same suddenly-opened trapdoor, and at the very same moment the smoothness of the bay splintered as a huge back emerged. It looked big enough to be the keel of a capsized ship, but before it sank out of sight, he glimpsed a gigantic fluked tail emerging with a flourish from the bubbling waters. Then it was gone. For a moment there was a paralysed hush, but it was followed by a huge baritone trumpeting note, which reverberated off the hillside opposite like a shout of triumph.

The people knelt, waiting, not moving.

The thunderous shout was still echoing from hillside to hillside when the whale showed itself again, hurling itself bodily out of the water. It was a sperm whale at least sixty feet long, and it shot vertically out of the water, reversed itself in an unhurried mid-air somersault, and returned into the sea nose-first. The somersault might almost have been sportive but for the monster's terrifying size.

After another moment's rapt silence the creature broke the surface again and spat a jet of spray from its blow-hole. The fetid fishy smell of its breath, which made him almost gag, and the sight of its back, seamed with glaring white scars and leprous blotches and trailing scarves of sloughing skin, made him sense a quite unselfconscious virile ugliness, a creature totally certain of its own immense strength and will: but it was not a limitless infinite strength and will, simply much, much greater than any human's, yet completely natural, completely finite, even somewhat brutish.

The whale wallowed on the surface for a full minute. It seemed to be inspecting the people lining the shore, though its tiny eyes, low down near the corner of its mouth, were not visible. Then, with a neat flick of its enormous tail, it disappeared.

The drumming started up again, but this time very raggedly, and the islanders began to drift back to their huts, some of them shouting and laughing among themselves, others walking apart and silent. Some rather dirty wooden bowls full of cooked rice, plantains and stringy chicken were placed at Imogen's feet, and some coconuts and a roasted piglet thrust into her arms by women who said nothing and immediately turned away.

Down at the water's edge two black dorsal fins cruised, like art nouveau periscopes, observing them.

XXX

They had passed beyond the frontier of the man-ruled world.

After thousands of years of man's enslaving animals, at last an animal species had enslaved man. The township in the bay was the whale's first political dependency on the human mainland: perhaps simply an experiment in the exercise of power.

From the very beginning the area west of Bermuda had had a sinister reputation. Passing through it on his first voyage to the New World, Christopher Columbus had seen strange lights and vast shadowy figures in the sky. During the years that followed a number of ships sailed into the area and were never seen again, even naval vessels like the 923-ton British training frigate HMS *Atalanta* which went missing in 1880, or the US Navy supply ship USS *Cyclops*, lost in

March 1918 with 309 men on board. At the end of the Second World War the malign influence of the Bermuda seas extended itself into the sky: five US Navy torpedo bombers on a formation flight from Fort Lauderdale disappeared without trace, as did the long-range flying-boat sent to look for them: no life rafts, no oil slicks or wreckage; a member of the subsequent Board of Inquiry said: 'They vanished as completely as if they had flown to Mars.' Over the next five decades several airliners disappeared in the area after inexplicably losing radio contact. The most celebrated such incident, subsequently immortalised by the Everly Brothers' hit single 'Ebony Eyes', involved the *Star Tiger*, a British South African Airways Avro Tudor IV, in January 1948: it had on board six crew and twenty-five passengers, including Air-Marshal Sir Arthur Coningham KCB, KBE, DSO, MC, DFC, AFC, wartime commander of the Desert Air Force and later of the 1st Tactical Air Force in North Africa, one of the most experienced aviators of his generation. The control tower at Bermuda received a radio message from the *Star Tiger* reporting that it would be landing on schedule: and it was never heard from again. Just under a year later another Tudor IV of British South African Airways, the *Star Ariel*, en route from London to Santiago in Chile with seven crew and thirteen passengers, disappeared shortly after a refuelling stop at Bermuda, having radioed its position about fifteen miles off the coast as it set course for Jamaica. The worst air disaster in the area was in February 1996 when a Turkish Boeing 757 en route from Trujillo to Frankfurt with 189 people on board plunged into the sea: its 'black box' was never recovered.

Books were written about the so-called Bermuda Triangle: campaigns were launched to get the police to institute regular patrols. It wasn't just the disappearances. There were strange lights, inexplicable electrical phenomena; compasses and radios did odd things; there was even talk of radioactivity, cosmic rays, and localised reversals of the ratio of negative to positive ions in the atmosphere. There were theories about submarine earthquakes, the lost civilisation of Atlantis, or visitors from other planets, perhaps even from other galaxies.

No-one suspected the whales, preparing their long counter-attack.

XXXI

The islanders took them to an empty hut on the headland, at the foot of the dead volcano, and brought them food every morning and evening, carrying away the dead policemen who were washed ashore on the beach in the night.

When he asked where they were the islanders began arguing among themselves in an impenetrable dialect that occasionally sounded like Spanish, and an old woman with a dirty bandage over her eyes began screaming and had to be dragged away. Next day a tattered old Philips school atlas was brought to them with their food. The page showing the West Indies had been torn out and subsequently fixed back in again with two rusty pins; it was crumpled, curling and yellowed, as if it had been soaked in urine and then left in the sun. Imogen turned to the page showing

South-West England: it was missing. They did not ask any more questions.

Each evening the bird that had followed them on the path down to the village would come and sing to them for exactly fifty-five minutes. It had a huge repertoire. Sometimes it sounded like a thrush. At other times it mimicked the bird calls they had heard during the day, the *o-kralee-o* of the red-winged blackbird, the wheezy chatter of the village weaver, the *ting-ting* of the grackle. One evening it faultlessly reproduced one of the contralto coloratura arias Imogen's pet blackbird had used to sing to them in their flat in Finsbury Park.

His various cuts and bruises healed quickly, though not as quickly as Imogen's: her skin was completely unmarked after only two days, as he noticed when she stripped off to go swimming. The mere thought of swimming in the whale-infested waters made him squirm, but Imogen pointed out that the whales were hardly likely to stoop to eating them now, after they had brought them safely all the way across the Atlantic. Since there was nothing else to do but eat and doze and throw pebbles at land crabs, he soon began to join her in the water. Anyway, it gave him an opportunity to chase her, attempt to duck her, swim under her, grab her by surprise, and so on.

Occasionally there seemed to be strange objects far

out to sea, catching the light on the sunny horizon, just below the frieze of clouds.

Though he slept by her side in the hut, she always seemed at her most remote and unresponsive in the late evenings; and whenever he woke in the night she opened her eyes immediately. But in the water she tolerated his horseplay, though her swimming improved so quickly that she was soon much more agile in the water than he was.

After they had swum, they would stretch out on the bright sand to dry themselves because of course they had no towels. He would lie there looking at her bottom and beyond it the ceaseless march and counter-march of the lace-fringed waves. The wetness of her hair caused it to cling close to her skull, parting in unfamiliar places, occasionally showing him the huge red scars where her head had been sliced open like a melon.

She was not unkind to him. She used to fetch the gourd of water, and fruit, after they had swum, and would show him sea-shells she found. She expressed disappointment at his ignorance about them, in a way that was obliquely flattering in that it implied that she had been counting on him to know everything; and she grinned delightedly when he held one of the shells to her ear so that she could hear the sea. The only response she made to his constantly staring at her nakedness was to tease him occasionally by striking a pose like Botticelli's Venus, with one hand over her breast-bone and the other over her thighs. And she patiently discussed his various schemes for stealing a boat and escaping, and told him – twice – how brave he had been in the jungle, with the jaguar. She even thought to ask now and then if he was bored.

He *was* bored. The islanders brought them food but otherwise kept away. They could smell the cooking fires of the township across the bay, and sometimes the wind also carried the sound of reggae to them: the islanders seemed to play a lot of reggae on their one or two beat-up cassette-players but occasionally he also heard 'You'll Come Back for Me'. But they had no other contact with the people, and nothing to do but laze in the sun and swim. In the evening clouds would gather, dove-grey with white highlights, and the two of them would watch their stately progress from nowhere to nowhere. He could not see what they were doing there, alone together on their holiday brochure headland.

And then, slowly, he began to understand.

One night, about an hour after midnight, he woke and found that Imogen was lying on her back beside him, eyes closed but evidently more than usually conscious. And outside, from out to sea, above the slow rumble of the surf, he could hear a strange, deep-toned clicking like a Geiger counter, occasionally varying in tempo and now and again interrupted by groans and whoopee-cushion noises. It was the whales, trying to talk to Imogen, talking to one another in the hope that Imogen, eventually, would Understand.

The following night he woke about eleven, and the groaning and clicking had already begun. There was almost a full moon, and the sea gleamed and caught the silver light, but there was no movement, only the bursting breakers like ghosts in the moonlight and the strange mouthings from beneath the waves.

Overhead there were millions of stars, millions of planets, perhaps millions of life forms: here there was himself, his robot, a conversation with the whales.

He remembered what 'The Professor' had said: that the artificial brains, because of their ability to reproduce their cells, had an almost unlimited and exponential capacity: they might develop psychic and intellectual powers far beyond the human.

'Go back to sleep,' said Imogen, opening her eyes. 'This is very difficult for me. I have to concentrate.'

During the nights that followed he slept without waking.

XXXII

Whales do not perceive themselves as autonomous individuals. They have no personal names. Each whale knows a host of individuals, being most closely involved with blood relatives. Stranger whales of the same species from other territories are rapidly assimilated into family-type networks. A whale perceives itself as in a family-type relationship with all the other whales of its acquaintance, and identifies the others by their role in the family. But as each individual has a different role in the family, the same whale is not thought of in terms of the same relationship by all the other whales it knows – just as, in a human family, the same man might be, to one, a brother, to another, a husband, to another, a son, to another, a father.

The whales have vastly more of these relationships, but there are no *nouns* to denote these relationships: each different relationship is associated with a huge vocabulary of *verbs* denoting different modes of relating.

While human culture has advanced through the interaction of communication and manipulation of objects, whales have no normal manipulation of objects and their everyday conversation is only concerned with communicating within relationships.

There are similar complexes of verbs to describe their interaction with other species, including their food, and with the sea, and with the weather.

The vocabulary to describe what is going on outside their immediate range of interaction, for example human behaviour (which is known to them only, as it were, at an immense distance), involves extremely complex problems of conceptualisation, and the learning of this vocabulary is a major intellectual threshold in a whale's existence, comparable to the learning of theoretical physics or the calculus for humans.

Because humans, even of very different and virtually unrelated cultures, respond to their material surroundings in essentially similar ways, it is possible for humans to learn to understand foreign languages; but humans and whales respond to their material surroundings in such fundamentally alien ways that the human brain cannot even begin to comprehend the linguistic universe of the whale.

But Imogen's artificial brain had long since ceased to be merely a human brain.

XXXIII

On the fourteenth day Imogen woke oddly convinced that *today* they would see a sign.

And at eleven o'clock they did.

They were at the side of the hut facing the township when they noticed the islanders beginning to gather at the sea shore. This time there was no drumming but they saw that the islanders were moving in a strange unison. They would all turn their faces left at the same moment or raise their right hands at the same moment. They did not stand in any particular order, and the extent of their gestures was not uniform, but they really were making substantially identical gestures at one and the same time.

And suddenly the wind seemed very strong, and huge mother-of-pearl clouds began to pile up and the sky was full of circling seagulls.

There was a single peal of thunder, like the crack of a starting pistol magnified a thousand times, and a rainbow curved in the heavens over the township, and the people danced in unison more and more rapidly, and it seemed as if their dancing was in time to the magnified crashing of the surf.

The mad symphony became faster and faster. The rainbow flicked out, wiped away it seemed by a low cloud, then came back newer and brighter, now a *double* rainbow, the sequence of colours repeated in a wider band. The palm trees tossed their fronds spasmodically and the circling seagulls shone with a strange radiance.

The earth began to tremble. The flimsy hut shook violently from something stronger than the wind. Oily black smoke spat from the top of the conical mountain that reared above them on their promontory. As they had thought, it was a volcano, but not an extinct one.

That was the whales' sign. They controlled the wind, the lightning and the sea, the thunders locked up in the heart of the earth, and the people on it.

*

After two more days Imogen confessed that she was 'learning things' but that it was difficult to explain.

'I'll tell you as soon as I can,' she promised.

She looked at him with that eager, ardent, round-eyed expression which the real Imogen had never had: eager, ardent, but puzzled, and searching both for the right words, and for the meanings behind those words, her face turned up so that the line of her throat and chin was clean, girlish, pure.

'I think this, somehow, is what I was *meant* to do. To learn to speak to the whales. It is for this that I came into existence.'

'You were brought into existence simply to be a specimen in a laboratory,' he said brutally, for without knowing why he was jealous.

'You don't understand,' she said, still ardent-faced, without even a flicker of hurt in her expression. 'There are purposes behind purposes.'

She turned away, and said, a little sadly, though he could not know if she was regretting past time wasted, or newly lost innocence:

'I don't bother to think *what* I am, I just *do*.'

Her voice sounded unnecessarily loud and emphatic in the momentary deep silence before the sucking roar of the breaking waves.

And then that ardent look again, but more confident.

'It's *you* who have helped me to this. I know it has been strange and terrible, but it's *you* who have helped me.'

She was so beautiful then: a splash of sun across her brown shoulder; sitting sideways with her feet tucked under her and the light glowing on the little parallel hairs of her thighs; leaning forward with a small boy's muscle knotting under the soft flesh at the back of her upper arm as she propped her weight on it, and the softness and tautness of her body an image of the yieldingness and strength of her femininity, and all of it focused in her face as she looked into his eyes. And he knew he was in love with her.

Love is awareness of another person's soul.

XXXIV

Most people assume they have had no existence previous to their birth, so why should they have continued existence after their death?

The notion that the life-span of a human being is part of a larger sequence, with death as the beginning of a period of reward or retribution, was familiar to the Ancient Egyptians. They believed that after one's death one was led before a panel of judges. Similarly the early Zoroastrians taught that the dead were obliged to cross Chinvat, a bridge over the gulf of Hell, which was narrow for the wicked, broad for the righteous. These concepts of eternal reward and retribution were grafted, along with the concept of expiation, on to early Christianity and thereby given a new lease of life, but from Albertus Magnus in the thirteenth century onwards Christian theorists focused increasingly on the notion that the individual's soul was undying primarily by virtue of the nature of its relation to God. During the following centuries, as the idea of God waxed and waned in its hold on the human imagination, the idea of the Individual, or at least people's sense of their own Individuality, became more and more emphasised. For many people during the last hundred years the idea of God was essentially a derivation from their belief in their own Immortality. It is no longer God that provides the chief argument for the Immortality of the Soul, but the individual consciousness's insistence on its specialness.

Imogen and the other Calloway Institute experiments, with their artificial consciousness – man-made but with the potential to become more-than-humanly unique – seemed to give the lie to this argument: for could an Immortal Soul be created in a laboratory guarded by armed police?

XXXV

She asked him:

'If you had the chance to ask one question which you knew would be answered, what would it be?'

She seemed to be on the brink of learning the answers to *everything*.

In the morning she would speak of what she had heard and half-understood during the night, and they would sit side by side, knees touching, or lie close enough together for outstretched hand to reach outstretched hand, and often when he looked at her he would meet her eyes gazing at him.

She paraphrased what the whales were telling her about the history of man from *their* point of view, and their perception of the variety of men: coastal men, men on rivers, men who had never even seen the sea and for whom the steppes they lived on were their idea of infinity. The whales hinted at explanations for long-familiar human actions. It seemed that the world was far different from what humans believed it was; and what humans thought was their free choice and initiative was part of an evolutionary process in which humanity was only one of a multitude of participants.

Although every species was interacting with every other, all species were impelled to evolve towards their own optimum. She tried to explain to him how even his determination to fight his own lonely battle against *if only* was part of an evolutionary struggle, his own working out of the principle of survival of the fittest – yet, she was not sure, perhaps even at the time he came to her at the Institute he may have been influenced by the whales. At any rate, competition was the principle of all change, all evolution in the world. And three species were in a race to be the first to evolve a *true* consciousness: man, whales, ants. The Struggle – the endless winter which the whales had launched, the epidemics bred by the ants – all that was part of the race, one round in a long contest. Apparently the ants did not mind man's murderous destructiveness – they had always practised mass-murder themselves – but hated man for having preceded them in gaining control of electricity and for having nuclear power. But they had learned much earlier than man how to modify biological species by genetic engineering and how to create organic life, like the viruses which were decimating the human species. The Greenland Right Whales, meanwhile, had a plan to capsize the earth in its orbit and tilt the equator further from the sun. The alliance between the ants and the whales was merely a temporary one. The only question was whether this alliance would end before or after the destruction of humanity.

There was something they had said which she had not yet quite understood, about the ants and the First World War, the war in which millions of men abandoned their industrial cities, the islands of sterile brick and concrete where they had been safe, and lived for four years in holes in the ground, digging into rich farmlands teeming with insects, tunnelling under the roots of trees where there dwelt life-forms which never saw the light of day, and leaving their dead in thousands under the hostile skies, to serve as food for flies and ants and rats.

'I don't think the whales *like* the ants,' she said.

She even told him a whale joke: The reason why we live far out at sea is that it is the only place we can keep clear of shit.

Then one morning all she had to say was:

'I *think* I'm understanding what they're saying. I'll tell you when I'm more sure.'

Later he noticed that her responses to his attempts at conversation were much more non-committal than they had been since their leaving London.

When he suggested a swim, she answered:

'*You* swim if you like.'

The villagers had left them a guitar on which she had taught herself to strum oddly recollected fragments of 'I'll Come Back for You' and other pop songs. She spent the afternoon plucking the strings as if at random, producing a slow, abstract, plangent music which haunted him uncomfortably.

He woke briefly that night, heard the whales calling to Imogen.

The next morning she hardly seemed aware of his presence. He had to ask whether she had made any progress during the night. She merely shrugged.

She ate ravenously, and after strumming the guitar for an hour, went for a swim on her own. She was away so long that he became worried.

'There's sharks out there,' he warned her when at last she returned.

'They couldn't harm me,' she said, without interest, combing out her bush of hair.

'What's the matter?' he asked pleadingly.

'Nothing's the matter,' she responded tartly. And from then on he knew everything had changed.

During the next few days he knew he had lost her.

She scarcely spoke to him. She swam, strummed the guitar, spent nearly an hour peeling a stick she had broken off a shrub, but mainly just sat on the beach, staring out across the waves. She did not answer when he tried to tease her, did not notice when he sulked.

At last he burst out:

'What's happened? What's changed?'

'I don't want to talk about it,' she said shortly.

It was as if she had withdrawn completely from whatever relationship they had ever had. And he was tortured by her withdrawal.

'I'm in love with you,' he told her. 'I don't know why I wasn't before. But I am now.'

She looked at him, with a vexed expression, as if obliged to ration every moment that she was not staring at the sea.

'You *think* you're in love with me,' she corrected him. 'You don't understand.'

What made it worse was that he could see she was radiantly happy. As she sat looking out to sea, clasping her knees, a little furrow between her eyes as if she was concentrating on the horizon, there was a kind of light within her, a glow not just of certainty or fulfilment but – was it this that made him jealous? – a glow of love.

In the evenings she sat with the guitar and played slow, eerie sequences of chords.

At last she explained:

'I now can understand the whales. I have learnt things that it was not possible for any creature to know before. I have found a *new* way to be human. I have learnt how far humans are acted upon, how far it exists for them to be actors, initiators, how far, to what extent, one can be free. But you humans aren't ready to understand it yet. One day. A long time in the future. *If* there's a future.'

That night the men from the township came to take him away.

In their last two or three minutes together he had her full attention to a degree he had never had before.

'I shall never forget you,' she said. 'I'm sorry you won't see our child – something *did* happen that night on the mountain, it wasn't a dream – but I'm going to name him after you.'

And the woman that had been Imogen Campbell raised her face, which glowed like a new flower, and for the last time her lips parted beneath his to take his kiss.

A NOTE ON THE AUTHOR

A.D. Harvey is well known to the readers
of leading American, British, Dutch, French,
German, Hungarian, Italian, Russian and Swiss
scholarly quarterlies.

A NOTE ON THE TYPE

The text of this book is set in Linotype Sabon,
named after the type founder, Jacques Sabon. It was
designed by Jan Tschichold and jointly developed
by Linotype, Monotype and Stempel, in response
to a need for a typeface to be available in identical
form for mechanical hot metal composition and hand
composition using foundry type.

Tschichold based his design for Sabon roman on a
fount engraved by Garamond, and Sabon italic on a
fount by Granjon. It was first used in 1966 and has
proved an enduring modern classic.